THE CHANGE MAGIC—

Like a creature out of ancient legend, Amant's pet teka leaped from his shoulder to the air. Amant chased after the teka as she soared across to the alder. He watched as she soared again and glided silently in circles around the tree. Suddenly, Amant wished that he too might soar. He wished he might join his teka in flight, angling on the wind and drifting smoothly in a perfect loop.

Amant ran. He felt the wind against his body; he held out his arms. Faster and faster did he go, following the teka, trying to catch up with her as she sped along the edge of the grove. The wind made his ears burn, brushed through his hair, and he laughed—but the laughter came out as "keir-ah!" and in the next instant, he had launched himself into the air! He was no longer human; his shoulders had sprouted wings, his hair had turned to fur. He was airborne, a teka, as fiery as any wild-spawn!

THE BOY WHO WAS THROWN AWAY

STEPHANIE A. SMITH

DAW BOOKS, INC.
DONALD A. WOLLHEIM, PUBLISHER

1633 Broadway, New York, NY 10019

First DAW Printing, January 1989

1 2 3 4 5 6 7 8 9

PRINTED IN THE U.S.A.

For Tone

Note:
A genealogy
of Trost's Servitors
appears at the back
of the book.

Contents

THE DARKNESS

He has not joined me yet,
peers from no mirrors.
My skull's my own, so far.

He is the other,
smiling from friends' eyes,
prince of the empty houses
and the lost domains behind me
and the last domains before me.

He is the brother
and the prince and the stranger
coming from far
to meet me; but we have not met.

And so I fear darkness,
            like a child
                    —Ursula K. Le Guin
                    from *Wild Angels*

1

The Boy-Who-Was-Thrown-Away

TO THE LAND of a thousand lakes, the boy-who-was-thrown-away returned. On foot, drenched by autumn showers, he walked down from Mt. Oron's pass to the lake valley alone. Today, in the Ebsters' Hall at Mossdon Kield, where the boy first discovered the great music in his soul, we say that he was no longer a child, but not yet a man, when he made that journey to the place of his birth—a journey that would lead him elsewhere, because we say too that he found no true home in the valley. And so, because his dearest, deepest wish was to find the place where he was needed, I would tell you a story, not only about the return but also about the home-finding of the boy-who-was-thrown-away.

Come along with me now, down the road to the lake valley and Bildron Kield! See it as it was once, in the long, long ago, in the time before the boy fathered the Reconciliation and became the finest orphic in all Gueame! See it as a muddy, rutted lane.

The boy walked down that lane speedily. He

was cold. The satchel strapped to his back pulled at his shoulders. He might have stopped to take the burden off, but he was impatient to reach Bildron. He was tired. It was raining hard. He wanted nothing more than to reach the encircling walls of the town. And, too, he was anxious, because he believed he would find his family in Bildron, his mother, his father, his aunt, and his young cousin, Osei. *O!* he wondered, *what will they say? Will they even know me?* It was twelve summers since he had been thrown away; he was not the same person anymore. He would be a stranger, with strange ways, alien to the valley Kield and valley folk. And yet . . . he was not so very, very changed—was he? Thus, he did not stop to rest, but hastened on, hoping that his people might welcome their missing child home.

As he approached the Kield, he stared at the formidable double gates of the walls, taller than a tall man's height and finished with elaborate brass fittings. They were fine and new, and strange because he remembered the old, pitch-soaked gates that had had no brass. He remembered how those old gates had been breached by the Tenebrian raiders on that night he was thrown away. The raiders had hacked a ragged hole in the planking. Black splinters of wood had littered the cobbles and—*O!*—he saw in his memory all the Kield burning. The yellow flame-tongues had crackled and writhed, and ate what was left of the gates. The foul odor of burning pitch had seared his throat; the billowing, acrid smoke had stung his eyes.

He walked closer. Bildron had been rebuilt so that no trace of the ruin showed; everything seemed as if no such raid had ever been. From his high vantage on the lane, he saw the crowded, newly built villas inside the walls. Roof tiles of indigo and bright carmine, polished by the rain, flashed when the sun rent a cloud, as scales shine on a leaping fish. Chimney spouts breathed woodsmoke. At the heart of the circular Kield, he spotted the twelve black and conical roofs of the Drake Villae's home, from which she ruled her valley. Yes, everything seemed as if no raid had ever been, except that the boy remembered. He could not forget.

He shivered, and as he walked down the hill, the Kield roofs shrank from view until he could see only the stone walls, the gates, and there, beside the gates, looking tiny indeed, the door to the porter's lodge. On the window grate of this door in the wall, there hung a bell. He rang it. A moment later, the porter peered out from the dim interior and said, "What do you want?"

The boy-who-was-thrown-away pushed the cowl off his head and wondered, *Should I ask after my family now?* But, afraid lest the porter not believe him, he said, "I wish a night's rest." And this was true enough.

"Where do you hail from, youngster? Whither are you bound?" asked the porter.

"I come from Mossdon Kield," said the boy. "I go to Kheon."

"Kheon? A long way."

The boy nodded. "The carrier to the Cape stops here? So I was told, in Mossdon."

"It stops here—in two eves time." The porter eyed the boy and coughed. "A long way, for a child alone to travel."

"So it would be, if I were still a child," said the boy. The porter laughed at this impudence and then disappeared from the window grate. The door was unlocked. But it opened such a little bit that the boy was obliged to squeeze himself inside. The lodge had been made of the same granite as the wall and mortared with the same skill. He saw a hearth and two windows in the first room; a short hall led to the rest of the lodge.

As he was bidden, the boy set his damp satchel at the hearthside. The porter took his jacket from him, brushing the rain off the fur lining. The boy-who-was-thrown-away shivered again. He stepped across the room to the two windows, which looked out onto the main street of Bildron—the only street in all of the Kielding that runs straight and does not wind about, even unto this day. The straight street heads directly to the heart of the Kield, where the water well stands and where the twelve-roofed villa of the Drake opens its door to visitors.

As the porter set a kettle over the fire, the boy peeked out at the street. He watched children dash past the distant well, on their way home from lessons—at least, he supposed that they were on their way home from lessons. The children charged across puddles, laughing and pushing one another. Some dawdled, despite the wet, and the boy was reminded of the time when he had been one of those dawdlers, shy of elders and always named small for his age. And, as he recalled himself, so too did he remember that day when his aunt had dragged him to the door of their home and threw him away. She had tumbled him down the red brick stoop and told him he was a fool.

Shall I speak of how my great-great-grandfather came to be thrown away? There are many different versions of this tale, but I know the truest one. In this I make no idle boast, because I speak the tale the boy himself did tell, when he had grown old.

On that terrible day when his aunt put him out the door of their villa, and tumbled him down the red brick stoop, she had cried, "Out, out, out! And when you can do more than sing or be lazy, then come back. Not before." She tossed his shirt at him and his abacus. She said, "Can't even learn to count proper!" She shook her head and turned her back on her nephew. "Don't come home until you can use that abacus proper!"

He stood and picked up his shirt and the abacus. His aunt marched unsteadily back up the stairs into the villa. She shut the door, making the silver bell on it leap and ring.

He ran after her and pounded on the closed door. No one answered. He stood on the stoop and begged his aunt to let him in. He beat on the wood with his palms until his hands stung, though his classmates laughed at him as they passed by, on their way to lessons. They called for him to leave off crying and come along with them. His aunt was known to be a little out of her head and she would no doubt forgive him by the end of the day.

Still, while the wind whistled and blew, scattering leaves and chasing the dogs off the streets to shelter, the boy kept on begging, making promises

to the closed door. And he did not stop because
he could hear his cousin, Osei, calling to him.
Little Osei, who was more a sister to him than
cousin—she rattled the door knob and she cried
for him. He was afraid that his aunt would lose
what small patience she had left if Osei did not
hush soon. He was afraid of his aunt when she
had drunk too much wine or beer. And so he
tried to make more noise than the girl, to cry
louder and keep his aunt's anger from reaching
her. He did not know what else to do.

Soon though, he heard nothing, neither Osei
nor his aunt. He sat down with his back against
the door. He had cried himself into hiccups. He
wiped his nose and took the abacus out of his
pocket. It was small enough to fit in his palm and
it had come from a Kield beside the White Sea.
His father had bought it as a gift, and had told his
son that the marvelously smooth, gray-stone counting beads were plentiful in this faraway Kield, so
plentiful that they were strewn for leagues upon
the coastal sands.

The boy stuck the abacus on the stoop by his
feet and frowned at it. He knew how to count! He
knew how to count proper! But he had not been
doing the task his aunt had set for him, when she
had caught him that morning. Instead of pricing
the apple wine they were to sell at market, he had
been measuring out the beat of a street jongleur's
song. The boy-who-was-thrown-away sat beside the
closed door all the rest of the day, hoping. But the
door never opened. He got colder and colder.
The stone bit through the seat of his trousers with
icy teeth. Finally, as dusk settled over the streets,

he got up and ran away, leaving his tears and his abacus behind. For a time, he wandered up and down the twisty, winding roads, looking for somebody he knew, yet too embarrassed to go to any of his friends' villas. He shied away from the few people he did see, because they were strangers. He wanted his mother and father; *why had they gone to visit grandpa without him?* He wanted them to come home. So, when the darkness grew and the street lamps were lit, he went to the gates of Bildron Kield, to await his parents' return.

He stared at the pitch-soaked gates and at the light in the porter's windows. Miserable and wet, he went and huddled among the town dogs that were crouched against the lodge wall. He wedged himself between the dogs and watched avidly for any sign of the carrier bringing his parents home.

A while later, he wondered what he would do if he had to live for the rest of his life on the streets of the Kield. *What if his father, Lent, agreed with his aunt? What if his mother, Seftenir, did not want a naughty child in the house? Had a boy ever grown up without a villa to live in and a family to take care of him?* He had never heard of such a one—except in the tales his father told about wild Aenan. All at once, he was afraid. Why? Because in those days before the Reconciliation, Kieldeans taught their children to fear wild Aenan. They had forgotten Aenan's beauty, his wild strength, his gentle music. They had forgotten why he was the beloved of their own protectress, Trost, the Lake Mother of Wyessa and mother of us all. To some, he seemed an ogre, and they frightened themselves with sto-

ries of his ill doings. The boy was afraid to think
he might be like Aenan.

The dogs shifted. Some woke. Restive, one
whined. The boy could see their eyes shining in
the dark. The rain fell, a soft sibilance in the
midnight stillness. He curled up closer to the wall
and nearer to one of the dogs. Warm, wet dog
smell surrounded him. He tried to imagine living
with the pack all the time. He thought he might
enjoy being like a dog. And then he remembered
that wild Aenan had had the power to change
himself into any creature he wished. For it was
told to the boy that Aenan was devious. In his
craftiness, he befuddled people by turning himself into a bird or a frog or some such animal. But
why he had practiced such deviousness, the boy
was never told. Indeed, at that time in the Kields,
children were never taught that the name of wild
Aenan's power was insight and that it was the
same power that the Lake Mother of Wyessa, who
grants all wishes, has. In fact, before the Reconciliation, most Kieldeans knew little about the insight
and feared it greatly. They even tried to forget
that the Lake Mother and her servitors used insight to perform the wondrous deeds of which the
Kieldeans were so fond. And they especially feared
Aenan because he was not a Kieldean; he had
been a stranger, an outcast. Many a lie had cropped
up about him.

The boy had been taught some of these lies, but
on that night, as he sat huddled in the dark with
the dogs, he thought to himself, *Well, if I must live
as wild Aenan lived, without family or villa, perhaps the
Lake Mother will grant me the insight too, as she grants*

her own servitors! And he thought how fine it would be if he could have short, furry ears and a curled tall like a dog. If he had insight, he told himself, then he would fashion a black nose and a tawny face for himself, with black eyes and a white chest. He would have fierce, white teeth. No one would recognize him, and he would allow no person near him—except Osei. He would snap and snarl and dash at the legs of his aunt, to scare her. Howling, he would run over the streets of Bildron, and Osei would run with him. Maybe she would be granted the insight, too! And perhaps he would go into the valley and across to the snowy heights of the mountains, where the immortal mendiri were said to live.

He dreamed of himself prowling the Kield's back alleys, bellying along the gutters, tail down, teeth bared. He dreamed of himself baying at the moon, as a wolf, while he climbed the snowdrifts of Mt. Oron. And, as he glared about him, feigning dogness, wishing indeed that he might become as a dog, he was touched for the first time in his life by the gift of insight with which he had been born, but had not known. In his legs and arms, he felt a peculiar sensation—a sort of watery, loose-jointed melting—and he saw, for one tiny instant, fur on his forearms where his shirt cuffs should have been.

The dogs shifted again, scaring him. He sat up. There came a terrible sound—a pounding, repeated over and over, like a drum of monstrous size. The beat seemed closer to the earth than thunder and twice as loud. Several dogs stood. Some paced. Some began to howl. The boy glanced

up at the starless sky, to see if the moon were full
or even if it were visible, for he knew strange
things were rumored to happen in the light of the
full moon. But no, the moon was smothered by
rain clouds.

Then, not a few paces from where he sat, the
gates of Bildron Kield were splintered. The wood
split, cracking in one, long crack. Pieces of the
gate fell into the street. Little chips flew about,
like slivers of the night.

The boy wanted to run. He wanted to scream
out. But he could find no voice—it had hidden in
the parched land of a frightened boy's heart. The
dogs all were howling now, but in an instant they
scattered. Two or three barked steadily as they
disappeared down the street. The boy hoped their
noise would wake someone.

The hole in the gate grew into an uneven opening, through which several people crowded. With
them they brought the oddest creatures the boy
had ever seen.

At that time, he did not know that these beasts
were called *ponkatiloneti* or, in our language,
equuilopes. He did not know that the narrow red
ribbons tied in so complicated a way about their
muzzles were halters, bridles, and reins, nor that
they could be ridden, as a mule can be ridden.
The beasts looked to him something like the sheep
he tended, but they were twice as large and of a
honey color, with thick curly coats. Beyond that,
the boy did not notice much else, because one of
the strangers had discovered him and had hauled
him before the others.

Without giving the boy more than a quick glance,

the strangers spoke among themselves. He might
have run off, for all the attention they paid him, if
the one who had found him would let go his grip.
Whatever it was these people said to one another,
or whether they spoke about him, he could not
say, because their language had no meaning for
him then. But the sound of this strange tongue
was so musical to the boy's ear that, at first, he
thought they were singing.

Before he could recover from this shock, he was
placed high upon the back of one of the honey-
furred animals. He sat there, straddling a heavy,
thatched blanket, while the man who had found
him mounted up behind.

And they rode.

If you do not know what it is like to ride an
equuilope, then it will not mean much when I say
to you that the strangers and the boy-who-was-
thrown-away rode through Bildron Kield. In these
days, now that the Tenebrian raiders raid no more,
many of us have ridden upon the back of a
ponkatiloneti, but in the long ago, Kielding folk
did not know how to tame these desert dancers.
There were some southern Kielding people who
knew what it was to ride a mule, and there were
even some who had ridden a horse—those graceful but sturdy creatures brought to Gueame from
the Alentine Isles in Drake Quedahl's time. Still,
neither of these beasts can move the way an
equuilope does. When it canters, the light-limbed
equuilope seems to dance in utter silence, because
its prancing feet are padded and not hooved. To
the boy, it seemed as if he were flying along the
narrow, winding road of Bildron, like the darting

swifts that tenant rooftops. The equuilope passed
house fronts and shops. It angled along the curv-
ing streets, up the alleyways. It never stumbled or
hesitated—a marvel to the boy, who did not yet
know that the man's will guided their passage, not
the beast's.

And so, on that rainy night, the people of Bildron
woke to a storm of Tenebrian raiders. We know
now that this was the last raid those warriors of
the desert ever made upon the settled Gueaman
lands because there was an illness among the raiders; it was the sickness of a way of life dying. The
children of the steppes were leaving the *dovai*,
their home, for the busy port Kields of Mossdon
or Adeo and from there, over the White Sea to
distant bourns. Abandoned slowly by its children,
the *dovai* could not continue. The people had no
answers for this slippage in their lives. They saw
their children mock them. They saw their num-
bers diminish. Each succeeding snow, the *dovai*
grew emptier; each spring, another child would
leave, gone to learn the ways of the Kieldings, to
become like the folk in the valleys, to become
ponoi, the ones-without-shame. And, so for a time,
the people took to an ancient custom of retribu-
tion and raided the Kieldings, stealing whatever
they could carry, as their ancestors had once done
in the lean times before Drake Quedahl vanquished
them. They sought vengeance not for hunger but
for an ill they knew no other way to fight.

The boy-who-was-thrown-away, however, wanted
no understanding of why these strangers had come;
all he could understand was what he could see—
that they brought fire and screaming and smoke

and blood. Mute before the terror, he sat on the back of the curly haired beast. He sweltered in the heat of the flaming villas. He listened to the stern singing voice of the raider who held him.

Suddenly, the sweeping stride of the equuilope carried the boy and the man past the boy's own home. Twisting around, the child saw that the door of the villa was closed tight and that all the windows were barred and shuttered. He hoped that the house would be safe. But the air was acrid with smoke and bitter with the taste of burning bamboo.

The raiders soon left the ruined Kield, to gather on the valley road and look back on what they had done. They had taken what they had wanted; they had broken the peace of the thieving *ponoi!*

The man carrying the boy-who-was-thrown-away dismounted. He lifted the child off the equuilope's saddle blanket to the ground. Holding him by the shoulders, the man knelt in the wet grass beside the child, eye to eye. He pushed aside the boy's amber-blond hair so that he might better see the slim, dark brown face, and he said, "What is your name?"

The boy stared dumbly. The stranger had spoken to him in his own language—how could that be? He was so startled that he began, at last, to cry.

Later, the boy could not remember if he had spoken his name that night. If he had, it was soon enough forgotten when the raider adopted the boy into his own kith, despite the other warriors' disapproval. On that day of his adoption, the child was given a new name—*Nowaetnawidef*, which means 'thrown-away-boy.'

That is the tale I heard from my great-great-grandfather about that awful raid on Bildron Kield. I know, too, that it was of the raid that the boy thought as he stood in the porter's lodge and looked out the window at the children in the street. He sighed and touched the rain-wet glass. The raiders had lost their *dovai*; his adopted parents had died; and he had not become the Tenebrian warrior he had dreamed of being, but rather a servant to the Ebsters of Mossdon and a chanter of songs. How that came to be, I will tell you in time. For the moment, let it be said that the boy shook off his memories as best he could and turned away from the window. He found that the porter was staring at him. He did not know what to say to such an intent gaze, so he sat down in the rocking chair beside the hearth instead. He held out his dark hands to the fire. He rubbed his fingers together, as if testing the nap of some soft fabric; indeed, the hearth's heat gave his cold hands as much pleasure as the touching of some fine silk might have given him.

The porter said, "How are you called?"

"In Mossdon," answered the boy, "I was called Nowa. . . ."

"Nowa?" said the boy's host. "One name? You are an Ebster?"

"No, no. I have been a servant to the Ebsters, and they named me. I do not have the proper kith to become an Ebster. But I am a chanter, and now I'm going to sing at the Academe." He paused, then said, "Tell me, do you know the family Wuulf-Moas?"

The porter's raised brows showed surprise. "I did."

"Did?"

"I knew that family . . . when there was still a family to speak of. If you have come to Bildron seeking their hospitality, child, you have come too late. They are gone. The villa is home to another now; Wuulf-Moas is no longer spoken here."

"Gone? But . . . where did they go?"

The porter lifted a steaming kettle from the fire and poured the water into a basin full of soiled clothing. After setting the kettle down again, the porter stooped and stirred the contents of a pot hung over the blaze. The boy smelled garlic and lamb. When his host drew the ladle out of the pot to cool a portion and taste, he saw a quantity of beans floating in the ladle's bowl. His mouth watered.

The porter said, "Why do you want to know where the Wuulf-Moas have gone?"

The boy hesitated in his answer. So much time had passed, *what if his host did not believe him?* But he had to know what had befallen his people, so he said, "They are my family."

The porter dropped the ladle back into the pot and straightened up. Eyeing the boy-who-was-thrown-away with a distrustful glance, arms folded, the porter of Bildron Kield asked, "How so?"

"Lent Wuulf and Seftenir Moas are my parents. Can you tell me where they have gone?"

"No," said the porter, stepping back. "And their son is dead. I . . . helped bury the child myself."

"Bury?" The boy sprang up from the chair and set it rocking backward, to hit the wall with a cracking blow. Of course his family thought he was dead! He had been missing too long, too long . . . but, who had they buried? he wondered. He made a vague movement toward his coat, as if he should grab it and run out into the Kield to find his house and his parents and tell them no, no, they had buried a stranger as their own. Yet, they were gone from Bildron! So the porter said. And what of little Osei? Where was she? Did she think, too, that he had died?

He glanced at where he had set his belongings down. Instead, he saw that the porter had backed away from him, holding the ladle from the soup pot like a club; hot soup dripped onto the floor. And the porter said, "Who are you, to come here and talk of the dead?"

The boy stared at the gray-haired woman with the ladle in her hand, as if he were surprised to find that he was not alone in the room. He said nothing, because there was nothing for him to say—how could he begin to explain that he was not dead?

She shook the ladle at him, spattering soup, and spoke again, in a voice that raised a chill up the back of his neck. "Who are you?" she demanded.

"Amant," he said. "Amant Wuulf-Moas. In Mossdon I was called Nowa, but Amant is my first name. My true name."

"I told you. That child is dead."

"No . . . no . . . please, you don't understand. . . ."

"I tell you," said the woman firmly, although her voice shook a bit, "I tell you the child is dead.

I buried my son, my little boy, in the long ago."
She glared at the one who stood upon her hearth's
stones, as if he were a noxious thing. "How did
you come to steal my son's name? Who are you, to
be so cruel?"

Amant stepped backward. He bumped up against
the rocking chair and sat down. He looked at the
woman, the porter of Bildron Kield, trying to see
his mother. He looked and looked, trying to find
the soft features he remembered inside the dry,
lined face of the grandmother who stood before
him, clutching a dented, blue-metal ladle and glar-
ing at him. He failed. She could not be his mother.

All of a sudden, the porter stepped up to him.
She peered at him closely with her green eyes, not
touching him, motionless. He thought she seemed
turned to stone, and he feared to disturb her, so
stern was her face and so tense her body. And, as
he sat in the rocking chair, staring back at the
porter, he began, strangely, to feel drowsy. Perhaps it was the heat of the fire, warming his numb
fingers and toes; perhaps it was the shock of what
the porter had revealed to him. Yet, perhaps it
was neither of these, but rather something in
Seftenir's gaze that made him want to curl up and
sleep. For, although not much is known about
Seftenir Moas, it is whispered that she bore a
touch of insight in her blood, and, like the Lake
Mother of Wyessa and her servitors, she could
look into dreams.

The boy-who-was-thrown-away closed his eyes.
He had made a hard journey out from Mossdon
and down through the Adeon Valley, past the
foothills of Mt. Oron, over Lake Wyessa, and then

through the lower mountain passes to Bildron.
His exhaustion and the stillness of the porter's
tiny, warm lodge (and perhaps the porter herself)
worked a spell of sleep upon him. He began to
think that he had dreamed of what the porter had
said. *Yes*, he decided, *it is a dream. This old woman
cannot be Seftenir. . . . Just as Osei comes to my dreaming, so am I dreaming now.* He began to think of
how many times he had dreamed of his sister-
cousin, dreams so real to him that when he woke
he was bewildered at her absence. How many times
had he wished to the Lake Mother of Wyessa, in
the secret places of his heart, that he might find
Osei again? Yet, he never had found her, and now
he might never, ever find her. Surely this dream
of the porter as his mother was as unreal as all the
rest.

The porter dropped her ladle back into the pot
with such a clang that it startled him out of his
drowsiness. He sat up.

She looked at the fire now, and not at his face,
as she said, "I . . . I buried him."

"But," whispered Amant, half-afraid to contra-
dict his host, yet unwilling to let her believe he
would cruelly lie, "I am Amant."

She nodded, as if in agreement. Then she said,
"I buried them both—Amant and his father. I laid
the one beside the other, gently, gently under the
tree. Lent died two short seasonchanges after the
little one . . . was taken from us." She sighed. "He
blamed himself, you see. Lent blamed himself for
leaving Bildron. We had heard rumors of the
Tenebrians. But my father was ill, and I wanted to
see him . . . *we* wanted to see him. I daresay Lent

blamed me, too. He blamed everyone, everyone
save the one who should have carried that blame—
his sister." The porter began to rock herself back
and forth. She did not look at the boy-who-was-
thrown-away, nor did she seem to know of his
presence. She spoke only to the fire and to herself.

"We heard of Giolla's cruelty," she said. "I heard
of it, from little Osei, when Lent and I returned to
a grieving Kield. O! Bildron was a piteous sight!
So many of the villas were burned. Doors pulled
off hinges here, and windows gaping there, and
the Drake going about the streets, by herself, unattended by her ci'esti. But the ci'esti were busy
nursing the wounded. Our old Drake would not
sit by while her people died. Not like her daughter, the Drake who rules us now—but, no matter.
Lent and I found our villa one of the few untouched. And when I saw it, I dared to hope that
all would be well. O! Did I not wish with all my
heart that the Lake Mother had guarded my family? But no. Giolla met us as we came in. The boy
was missing. My boy, my own, my only child. . . ."
She folded her hands tightly against her stomach until the knuckles showed white. "Giolla never
admitted to having locked him from his home on
that day. All Bildron knew it, yet she said nothing
herself. Poor Lent, he let her keep her silence
with him. And when his heart gave up on him and
the Lake Mother came to guide him to Death's
abode, did his sister grieve? No. She disappeared.
She went from Bildron the very night he died and
took her daughter away with her, too." The porter shook her head. "We found Amant outside the
walls. He and two others. Just children. Lost chil-

dren . . . killed so young. I told you, I helped bury
them. Lent and I buried the child where he had
fallen, under the alder tree. And, not long after
that, I buried the father near his son." Abruptly,
she turned from the hearth and went into another
room, shutting the door behind her.

Bewildered, Amant sat in the chair. He did not
follow her. The porter was his mother. Yet, he
could not quite believe it. He remembered Seftenir
as a lithe, blond woman with mahogany skin and
eyes the lively color of moss in the rain. She had
been a wine-maker's daughter and a wine-maker's
partner, not a gray old gate-porter with wrinkles
in her cheeks.

He looked around the lodge. It was a crowded
place, full of dried herb bundles that hung from
the hearth and shelves. Pots and spoons and a
profusion of knives lined one wall. A rickety
wooden cabinet held plates and cups. The caning
of the chair he sat in had broken in places. There
was a basket full of bone needles, spools of thread,
and scraps of cloth in a corner alongside a backstrap
loom strung with a narrow belt of woven stuff—all
of it, and the warm, damp odor of the stone, the
sweet, musty smell of the herbs, and the aroma of
cooking food reminded him not of his childhood
in Bildron (which seemed more a dream), but of
the *dovai.*

What was the fabled *dovai* like? Not many remember it. I have heard it said that its winding
passages have long ago filled up with the unkind
soil of the steppes. My great-great grandfather
told in songs that the *dovai* was built all underground, a vast nest of rooms attached to one an-

other under the yellow earth by crawl-tunnels—a
honeycomb community, an ant's hill of people.
Each family had its own cluster of rooms. Whole
kith lived side by side, hidden from the harsh
weather of the steppes. The *dovai* was a warm and
crowded place to live he said, especially when all
the people would gather in one room, the Telling
Room. There, curled up on the floor, they would
listen to the Tenebrian orphic Mathisianii Lo Dianti,
sing the *Song of the Making*—the *Haaimikin Oide*
—which no Kieldean had ever heard, before
Amant.

Thus, as the boy sat alone in the porter's lodge,
he thought of his childhood in the Tenebrian,
while he sought a clue to his childhood in Bildron.
Still, there was nothing in the lodge that spoke to
him of the past. There was not one thing that had
a familiar face, including the porter herself.

Suddenly, he had a queer notion that perhaps
he was not Amant. Perhaps he was a spirit of
himself . . . he had heard of unhappy spirits.
Mathisianii had spoken of such ones, ghosts who
returned from the Sea of Sansel's Net to haunt
the places they had loved in life. Could he be such
a one? This thought got him out of the rocking
chair. He put on his coat. He would leave and
take a bed in the Kield somewhere and get a little
sleep. By morning, he would know better who he
was and what to do.

However, before he could get himself out the
door into the Kield, the porter reappeared from
her bedroom. He put his satchel back down and
turned to look at her.

As if she had heard his thoughts, she said, "I

offer you my hospitality until the carrier comes, if you so wish. If not, I will take you to the Drake's villa. There are beds in her home for travelers, and I am sure she would welcome a young chanter, on his way to the Academe."

She spoke with such formality that, in return, Amant gave her a formal bow of acceptance. He said, "If you would, I prefer your hospitality to that of the Drake's."

She nodded and returned to tending the supper. He took off his coat again, as she shared out the stew between them. They ate in silence. Oddly, this silence was not at all disturbing to the boy-who-was-thrown-away and so he did not break it, even while he cleaned the dishes, even when his host showed him into a third room, across the hall from her own. She bade him a good eve and a good rest.

2

The Porter of Bildron Kield

S O IT WAS that my great-great-grandfather returned to the place of his birth, only to find himself called a name-thief and to find the boy whom he had once been, dead.

He closed the door of the bedroom. It was a tiny place, nearly a closet, occupied chiefly by a rigid-heddle table loom. The hearth had been kindled and a hasty pallet made up for him.

Alone, he sighed and sat down on a stool beside the hearth. He could hear the porter still moving about the lodge. Slowly, he undressed. He draped his trousers, embroidered vest, and shirt across the fender before the fireplace. The clothing was damp in patches from the rain. It was as weary looking as he felt, soiled and sad from his hard journey into the land of a thousand lakes.

Being a chanter of songs, the boy-who-was-thrown-away wished he might play some music for himself before he slept, to calm and quiet his uneasy soul. But he had left his satchel, and thus his instrument, in the other room. He did not have the strength, he felt, to face the porter again that eve; so he contented himself by singing in a whisper. What it was that he sang, I do not know. Its name has been lost to memory by the passing of many a seasonchange. I like to think that he sang a lullaby, a Tenebrian lullaby—perhaps the *Song of the Little Owl*—and that it eased his heart.

At last, he hopped onto the hard pallet and lay down, tucking the blanket around him. He turned from the firelight to the whitewashed wall and closed his eyes. After a few moments, he tried to picture to himself his parents' villa as he remembered it. In his mind's eye, he took himself through the house, room by room, step by step, searching in every corner for a key to the porter's face, something tangible that would tell him this woman was truly his mother.

He ended his search in the room that he had once shared with his sister-cousin. He and Osei had played for hours together there, early in the morning. Between them, they had six toys: his abacus, her reed flute, his stuffed bear, her stuffed owl, his violin, her chalk and slate. Sometimes, they would teach the owl and the bear the lessons that Amant had learned—Osei had been too young to go to lessons. But even so, she learned what he had taught her and she read his books. In fact, she sometimes scared him with her precociousness. They would often play music together—songs he had written or tunes she had made up and would hum to him. Sometimes, they would pretend that they had been born in a far-off land; maybe it was an island in the White Sea, or perhaps it was in distant Kheon Kield. Maybe it was on the beach from which the pebbles of his abacus had come, a place to which the two of them would return someday, to play music every morn and all the nights, and never have to do any chores.

Osei watched him whenever he played the violin, her pale brown eyes intent upon his hand. Her own fingers would twitch with annoyance if he made a mistake. She used to swear to him that her owl flapped its wings and that the bear rolled about on the carpet whenever the two children sang together. But he never saw such a thing and called her silly for making up such a story. Yet she would insist upon the truth of her story so much, that he often would watch the owl and the bear surreptitiously, waiting to see them dance.

Amant sighed and yawned. Thinking about the past made him sad. He opened his eyes, pulled the blanket up, rolled over—and saw a curly-haired girl, sitting on the edge of the pallet at his feet. She was Osei.

He tried to sit up, but his arms would not move. The blanket felt as heavy as stone. Osei smiled at him and folded her legs under her. She was no longer a child; she had grown, just as he had, but even so he knew her—those bow lips and her dark, thick hair, her amber-brown skin and those large, long eyes were hers, except that they were of a strange color, almost no color, nearer to white than her usual pale brown, or at least far different from those he recalled. She wore an odd garment too, like none he had ever seen her wear before, even in his dreams. It had sloping shoulders and wide sleeves. Over it, she wore a sleeveless robe. Both the garment and the robe were black. Something about it felt familiar, but he did not know what.

Osei closed her oddly changed eyes and started to sing. He smiled because he knew the tune. It was one of his own, one he had made up when they both had been little, and so he sang it with her. . . .

. . . .And then the boy-who-was-thrown-away woke up. His own voice woke him, for he was humming to himself the end of his old baby song. He coughed and pushed the blanket off him.

"Osei?" he murmured, although he knew it had only been another of his dreams. He clenched his fists. Ever since he had been taken away from Bildron, he had dreamed of her. Sometimes, he saw her as a child, sometimes older. Often, she would make him promise to find her. He would promise. Then, he would wake in tears because he believed he could not fulfill such a promise. How could he leave the *dovai*, he would ask himself, and set out across the steppes alone? Later, after he had become a servant to the Ebsters, he had been told that runaways would be maimed, if caught.

The other children of the *dovai*, when they heard about his dreams, had called him *dowanaten*, which means 'haunted.' They thought it a fine thing, indeed. To have ghost-dreams meant, to them, that a person was favored by wild Aenan's power, that power which Kieldeans feared and called insight. To the people of the steppes, there could be no higher praise because they revered wild Aenan and the *Haaimikin Oide* as the sole truth about the world, just as we revered the Lake Mother and

the Tales of Kheon, in those days before the Reconciliation, before everyone understood that the
Oide and the Tales are two halves of a whole.
However, Amant-Nowaetnawidef did not agree with
the praise of his *dovai*-kith; mostly, Osei's dream-
ghost made him lonely. Mostly, he wished she
would leave him be. In a certain way, he too
feared the *dowanaten*.

Amant sat up on the hard pallet. He felt dizzy,
and his head ached. Yet, he did not want to sleep
again, partly because he did not want Osei to
return and partly because of the song he had been
humming when he woke. He hummed it again.
Osei's ghost had sung words to the music, but he
recalled only the melody. It was simple, the melody, yet there was a purity to it he had forgotten.
The years of his training in Mossdon had made
his own songs seem crude. As servant to Ebster
Oeta, Amant had heard the music of the great
orphics, those who could create music from their
own hearts, those whose lives were made of music.
Amant learned that, among the Ebsters, there had
lived many a great orphic but that some of the
most revered had been raised in other lands, in
other Kields, and even as far away as the Alentine
Isles. He had listened to the rigid-patterned choral pieces written by the Ebsters to recount the
history of Gueame, from the first Kield-maker to
the Quedahl Drakes of his time; he had heard
thundering responsories served up by the Ebsters'
choir. He had often watched the sun set to the
raucous, uncouth wail of the chanters' woodwinds,
as they struggled to learn harmony and balance.
He often wished that he had been born of the

proper Mossdon kith to become a chanter in the choir, at the very least. But no, he was a servant, an outsider; he was forbidden. And, surrounded by the solemn, sacred music that is the Ebsters' lifeblood, even unto this day, the little songs he had made in his babyhood had gotten lost, as pygmies in a giant's forest.

Yet, those same tunes had once caught the attention of the Ebsters, thus saving the boy from slavery in a faroff land. It happened this way: In the terrible, frozen winter season of the steppes, the people of the Tenebrian used to burrow into their *dovai*. They would seal themselves up underground, surviving on stores set by in the warmer days. Now, during the winter of Nowaetnawidef's twelfth year, corsairs from the south came in the middle of the night, even as the Tenebrian raiders had come into Bildron when the boy was five. The corsairs—bandits as we know, Kielding folk who defy the Drakes' rule—were few in number but they caught the Tenebrians by surprise. Sealed inside the *dovai*, they had thought themselves safe and well-hidden, as indeed they had been for more years than any could remember.

Of that nightmare night, Nowaetnawidef remembered far too much; seldom would he speak of it, though he dreamed of it often enough. In his dreams, sometimes, he could not tell whether he was in Bildron or the *dovai*—the screaming, the smoke, and darkness, it all seemed to be one moment and the emblem of his life. Corsairs, or Tenebrian raiders, it did not seem to matter, the dying and the screams were the same. Again he was pulled away from his parents' side, again his eyes watched his home burn. The corsairs dug into the *dovai* and took the children, to sell; they left the rest dead, or dying, on the empty, frozen land. Or so they thought; some did survive, many more, in fact, than Amant ever did know. The reprisal they took much later upon the corsairs is legendary, but that story has no place here. So, in time, was the *dovai* rebuilt, and the people of the steppes live on—but I have never seen them myself though I am of their blood.

The corsairs took their booty, a string of twenty children, into Mossdon, where they were sold to slavers from the Alentine Isles. One by one they were sold, sometimes two or three at a time. Nowaetnawidef watched his brothers and sisters taken away; but none would take him. Why? He heard a buyer say, "That scrawny one? He is no desert son. Look at him! Little and black and sullen. He seems to me more like a northerner, and for stealing a Kielding child, my friend, you could bring the wrath of some Drake down upon me. No, thank you."

Finally, he was left all alone in the straw of the slavery pen, and so he began to sing to keep himself from tears. Two men stopped and listened. It was dawn; the boy had not eaten in two days and supposed that the awful people with the hard faces who had done this thing to him would just as soon have him follow his adopted mother and father to the Sea of Sansel's Net. He did not notice the two men who listened to him as he sang. One of them left, but returned in a moment; he climbed into the pen and carted Nowaetnawidef off from the wharves, up to the Ebsters'

Hall. The man, who was an Ebster named Oeta, made the boy his servant but treated him as a son . . . all because of one melancholy tune.

Amant got up from the pallet and sat naked beside the loom, before the smoldering hearth. He allowed the simple melody from his past to dance in his head as it would. He discovered that it preferred to sing to him in a viola's rich, dusky voice rather than in human words, as Osei had sung it. Then, a flute, a reed flute introduced itself. It trilled a counterpoint. Soon, its voice was doubled by a second, deeper flute, a bass flute, until that deep voice leaped into the harmony and shadowed the viola's throaty whisper. As the theme ended, it was the lighter flute's voice last heard, persistent and sad.

The boy-who-was-thrown-away stood and paced. Once, he glanced out the window. Night lingered at the edges of the day. The smudged glass panes, tiny as they were, changed their black hue to charcoal and then to a blue-silver, as the light changed from uncertain to shy, and finally to bold. In this chill, smooth, autumn dawn, the boy paced to the smooth, chill autumnal singing of his imaginary reed flute. The melody rose higher, extending the original theme beyond that first, fierce, and darkened verse that had danced inside his dream on Osei's tongue, as clear and as vivid as fire.

A whistling creak and the settling of metal on metal—the sound of a door latch being undone—broke the making of his song. The boy jumped, stung by that intrusive noise. He crept to the door of his room and put his ear to it. He heard footsteps on the other side, wooden heels on stone—a loud tread that was somewhat hesitant, as if his host were at least attempting silence. He put his hand on the latch to his room's door and depressed the tongue slowly until the door swung inward against him. He peered out. His host had dressed herself in a long cloak. She wrapped her head in a shawl, took two buckets from the rickety cabinet, and went out into the Kield.

Amant closed his door again and dressed. He left the small room as he had found it and went to the hearth where he had put his satchel. From the satchel, he took a long, wooden box. On the box's lid, inset, was carved a winter tree, made of redwood. The tree was leafless, knobbily rooted and knottily branched. He opened the box and lifted his viola out from its black plush lining. He put the instrument to his chin and tuned it, adjusting the strings to their proper tautness and absently playing scales or snatches of music he had learned in the Ebsters' service, to get at the sweetest tuning.

Suddenly, he let his fingers leap from the snatches and scales, into the heart of the theme that he had been making that morn. The viola gave sonorous voice to this harmony of his childhood, and the song gave substance to a past he could no longer see. Entwined with the strings' dark voice, he heard the counterpoint of the flute, though no flute truly played. The imaginary trill darted and looped about in his mind, now with an easy grace, as a bird in an updraft, gliding, now with a nervous, hectic flutter, as a bat fleeing daylight.

He listened to his music and waited to hear the bass flute of his imagination join him and so he did not notice when his host returned. Neither did he see her set the water buckets down, nor did he feel her standing beside him.

"Stop," she said.

He did so, lifting the bow off the strings with a lurch of surprise. The silence, so sudden, was like a mute gasp. Hastily, he put the viola in its box and tightened the bow string.

The porter of Bildron Kield touched the instrument, running her fingertips lightly up the strings to the tuning pegs. Without looking at Amant, she said, "My son once had something like this—smaller and not so well-made. Would you see it?"

The boy-who-was-thrown-away nodded.

She smiled, her gaze still on the viola. Then she went into her own room. In a moment, she returned with a sack, tied up with a frayed cord. She undid the knot and took out a violin.

The bow had no string and the instrument had only two left, but he knew it. He knew the dark wood, the fretted neck, and the tuning pegs. His violin. His own. And, seeing the instrument that had belonged to the child he had once been, Amant knew also, with no doubt, that the woman who held the violin was his mother. She was gaunt and gray; but now he truly saw that her eyes were still moss-green, and that the angle of her sharp nose, the deep, almost sleepy eyelids, and the full lips, these and all her face were familiar and belonged to him as much as the violin did. Or rather, he belonged to her, as much as any child might feel a part of his parents.

The porter of Bildron Kield closed the sack over the violin and left the boy to himself. He let her go without speaking since, once again, what could he say? If she did not choose to acknowledge him as Amant, he could not use words to make her see him. No words had that much strength. His eyes burned, but he did not cry. He felt like a ketch with no wind in the sails, or a merchant's brigantine full-stocked with precious cargo but having no place to go. Seating himself in the rocking chair, he waited, blinking dry eyes and trying to breathe evenly. But the porter who was his mother did not return. Her door stayed shut.

At last he stood and looked out the windows at the Kield. No children were beside the well now. The sun was high, although the sky was overcast with dark clouds. The street shown slick with the morning's rain. He leaned his forehead against the cold glass, watching the few pedestrians hurry along the roads, hugging themselves to the villa walls to get away from the strong wind and needling rain. The glass cooled his skin; he could feel the wind pushing against the window.

What should I do? he wondered. The porter's lodge was hot and too quiet for him. He grabbed his coat from a pegged board and left the place, going out into the Kield. He pulled the furred cowl up and, with his head down against the rain, walked.

At a side street he turned, letting memory take him where it would. The road was curved, narrow and darkened by the lowering stormy sky. Few people passed him. One or two looked at his face with curiosity of their own, because the street he had chosen was lined with villas and little trafficked, except for those who lived there. He was a stranger. He felt out of place.

Then, ten paces away from one villa, he stopped and stared. The red brick stoop, the two-story, red brick villa, and the tall, bamboo-shuttered windows—home. He walked up to the iron gate. As with the Kield itself, little here seemed to have changed; even the same silver bell hung upon the door. He looked about him. The street was empty. The villa looked empty, too. Hesitantly, he opened the iron gate, climbed the stairs, and sat upon the stoop. From the pocket of his vest, he took out an abacus. It was not the one his father had given him; that had been lost, along with his childhood, on the day he had been thrown away. In Mossdon, as servant to an Ebster, he had been given another; he stared at the abacus as the rain wet its counting stones, turning them from a tan to a dark brown. Idly, he pushed the stones back and forth, listening to the tiny clinking sound they made and trying to match that sound to the pattering of the rain on the pavement.

The silver bell jingled and the door above him opened. Amant jumped, as if he had been caught stealing. A man stood on the stair. He said, "A good morn to you! Is there someone here you have come to see? One of my daughters, perhaps?" Smiling at the man's easy manner, Amant shook his head.

"No? Pity. Something I might do for you, then?" The man stepped down, pulling his heavy coat around him. He was a big man, tall as well as rotund, and his coat buttons had trouble meeting their buttonholes.

"I thought," said Amant, "that this was the villa of the family Wuulf-Moas."

"Ah!" said the man, nodding. "So it was, once. You should have asked the porter. She could have told you that the family is gone from Bildron. You are new to our Kield, yes? Visiting? And you saw the porter. Did you speak to her at all?"

"A . . . a little."

"Well!" said the man, clapping his hands together. "She would know more than I. She is Moas. I bought the villa from her, before she became porter. The rest of them went away—to Kheon, it was thought. Giolla Wuulf was said to have had family there. But you ought to speak with Seftenir. She would know better than I."

"Seftenir," said Amant.

"Seftenir Moas, the porter, as I told you. . . ."

"Yes. Yes, I know," Amant said. "Thank you." He looked up at the villa that was once his home, but that was now no more a home to him, just another villa on a street of villas in a small Kielding of the valley Bildron. It was nothing to him. Nothing . . . except that it was in his memory, every room, every wall, every peg. And in that memory, he could hear his father calling to his mother, "Seftenir, Seftenir," gently calling her to join him on his evening walk.

"Where do you go?" said the man to the boy. He gestured at the street before them.

"Go?" Amant turned away from the villa. "To the Drake, I think. I have some . . . business, with the Drake."

"Do you? Well, youngster, when the business is done, if you would have a fine supper, come to the Owl's Pocket. Myself and my daughters, we serve a fine meal, and not expensive, only half a linganuli." He laughed and walked out to the street, holding the iron gate open for the boy. Amant followed him. Together, they went back to the well at the center of the Kield. The man pointed across the well and said, "The Pocket is on Blue Alley, near the wall." He glanced at the boy. "When you have done with the Drake, take a fine supper with me."

Amant gave the man a bow and thanked him again, promising to visit when the day was done. And the man went off whistling, leaving the boy alone at the Drake's villa in the rain.

Amant looked up toward the second-story windows and thought of the many ci'esti who lived inside, behind those windows. The ci'esti are the eyes and ears of the Drake; they are the children of her training, who did her bidding in the long, long ago, and who do her bidding now.

Did you know that the boy-who-was-thrown-away had almost become one of the ci'esti? Indeed! I heard this story from my grandfather, who heard it from his mother, and it goes this way: Once, when Lent Wuulf lost his temper, he said to his little son, "O, that . . . that we had given you to the Drake, as she wished! She would not have put up with your games! The ci'esti would teach you not to be so troublesome!" But, perhaps this is not a true story. Perhaps it is mere fancy, as so many of the tales spoken about the orphic Amant Wuulf-Moas are. Still, whatever the truth, everyone knows how fierce and strong are the ci'esti. In Bildron, people say, "May your wishes have the iron of a ci'esti's heart." Certainly, their reputation must have caused the boy to sigh deeply as he stood before the twelve-roofed villa. He knew he had to present himself to them because, only through them would he gain the ear of the Drake. And this, after all, was one of the reasons he had come to Bildron—to play music for the Drake and, at long last, to be in hiding no more!

As I have said, in Mossdon, the boy-who-was-thrown-away was Ebster Oeta's servant, a slave-bought child, supposedly a raider's brat. Since he had no Mossdon parentage and no Kield wealth, he was barred from the Ebsters' teachings and could not join the choir. However, despite this law, Oeta had tutored his servant in secret because he saw the child's talent. When the boy had grown old enough to take care of himself, Oeta gave him freedom from his servitude and sent him on a journey, the one of which I am now telling you. Oeta would have his pupil study at the school where he himself had once been taught, briefly, before he had become a full Ebster—the Academe in Kheon.

"Kheon—the largest Kield in all Gueame," Oeta said to the boy-who-was-thrown-away, after they had finished their last lesson together. "You should take a ship, as I did the one year I left Mossdon. It is quicker, safer, and more beautiful."

"But I must go to Bildron," said the boy quietly. "I must go home."

"Well, of course," said the old man. "I understand. And in Bildron, you can try to gain audience with the Drake, as practice before you reach the Academe. But there is nothing so lovely as

sailing into the port of Kheon, with the dawn."
Oeta folded the long sheet of music and tied it
into a sheaf with a ribbon. He took a second sheaf
and folded it, and picked up a second ribbon. His
large hands had a slight tremor to them. The
tremor made the ribbon capricious; temperamen-
tally, it eluded the knot. Oeta continued, "Kheon
is a marvel, or so I remember. And the Academe
there, why, that is a marvel, too." He secured the
knot and patted the folded sheaf. "Although I
have heard many a beautiful piece of music written here, sung by the choir or given voice by our
old and our young, still never has music been so
sweet as it was when I studied at the Academe.
Sweet . . . and difficult! The orphics worked their
pupils to the bone." He eyed the boy and folded
his arms. "You have much to learn. You haven't
had the proper sort of training here, and you will
be working twice as hard as the others in Kheon,
that is, if the Academe still exists."

Amant nodded and said quietly, "If it exists, I
will study there. Somehow."

Oeta sighed and sat at his desk. He was a big
man. The desk looked fragile next to his thick
arms and chest. "I have given all that I could. You
must leave. I see that."

Amant glanced over at his teacher. "You wish
me to stay? But . . . you said. . . ."

"Of course I prefer you stay! Child, you've been
a boon to me and a joy to teach." Again, the old
man sighed and shifted in his chair, making the
cane creak. "But I cannot turn my servant into
even a chanter here, much less an orphic or Ebster!
I cannot give you kith-ties, not even to my own

kith, not here—so they have told me again and again. What can you do in Mossdon, with the music you have inside you? Become a jongleur, travel from tavern to tavern, singing for bread? In Kheon, you will have a chance to become more than a servant. You will write music, as you should. Here, you would always be working in secret, either within the confines of my apartments, or perhaps in some dark hole of a villa. And you would never truly be free; too many here believe that you are a Tenebrian, a raider's child; too many would not care to know that you are from Bildron; too many would be jealous of your talents. In Kheon, you will be my nephew. I will tell the Academe that you are my nephew, come to study. As, in many ways, you are."

The boy did not know what to say to his teacher, who had just given him such praise. And praise beyond his hopes! To be Oeta's nephew! To be called kith to an Ebster family of generations! It frightened him. He closed the lid of his viola case and shut the heavy drapes over the shuttered windows. The winter cold haunted the floors that night, sneaking through crevices and icing the walls. Amant shivered and poked life into the fire. He wondered how he might thank Oeta properly, but the words stuck in his heart and would not come out.

The Ebster, meanwhile, cleared some staved paper from his desk top and unlocked a little door in the desk. The door hid a compartment stuffed with sealing wax and seals. He took a blue wax stick from a jumble of half-melted ones and lit the wick with the flame of his lamp. Holding the wax over a folded letter, he said, "Take this to the Academe. My name and this letter should do well for you." Again he sighed. "I don't believe that my old friend, Emrack Lizatial, is still living; I heard a rumor of illness and then nothing more, and so I fear the worst. But should he be there, or should one of his students be teaching in his stead, you would do well to study with him." He pressed his seal into the bubbling wax.

Amant put the letter in his viola's case. He felt new inside, so elated that he was not sure he could do anything but grin for the rest of that evening. He had heard so much from Oeta about the Academe and Kheon Kield, how they were free and wild and beautiful! Built on West Rock Cape, Kheon, like Mossdon, is a port town, although their climates are very different, Mossdon being an eastern Kield and Kheon being of the west. In those days, Kheon boasted a fleet of brigantines that sailed daily to other islands in the White Sea. Artists of all kinds—orphics and painters, potters and dancers—came from many foreign lands to visit Kheon. One such traveler had built the Academe as a school where musicians of Gueame might study the art, outside the rigidly sacred confines of the Ebsters' Hall. Ebster choirs were stunning—as they are still—and their praise for Trost, the Mother of us all, full-hearted, but they had no room for the new or the different. In the Academe of Kheon, the new and the different flourished.

Oeta leaned back in the chair and stared at his pupil. The Ebster had remarkable eyebrows, tangled as a briar thicket, white and gray-haired, they grew upward, away from his blue eyes, to make him seem always and forever astonished. He stared out from under the bramble of his brows and said "One more thing."

The boy turned from the hearth. He had been thinking of Kheon . . . but also of Bildron Kield; his journey would take him to his lost home.

Oeta said, "Nowa?"

And the boy gave his teacher a bow to signify that he was listening.

Oeta nodded. "Hear me, then, as you might hear a song I would have you remember. You may never hear what I have to say again, from me or anyone else. I would have you know it, before you leave me. You are more than a chanter, even now. And will be more in time to come. You are an orphic."

The boy held his breath for a moment. Then, he said, "One day, I hope to earn that name."

"Nowa." The old man pushed his chair back from the desk and walked across the room to his music stand. "You are an orphic already. I have heard the songs you have written, both those that I asked you to make and the ones you have made on your own and sung when you thought I was not listening. Only orphics can write music the way you do now: cleanly, beautifully, and with all their hearts. That you still have training to take— and the cold water of Kheon's ways will be most instructive, I have no doubt—is of little matter. Already you do more than simply sing or mimic, which is the art of the chanter. That you will not be an Ebster is also of little matter, to my mind." He glanced at his hands. "The greatest orphics have seldom been part of the kith, no matter how much the Ebsters say otherwise. Our talents have worn thin, and I wonder if the Lake Mother no longer favors us or our old ways. I tell you this because you may never know it again, except in the chambers of your own heart. If you come to doubt the beauty you are vessel to, child, I task you now to remember an old man's words."

"I remember," said the boy-who-was-thrown-away, as he stood in the rain of Bildron at the Drake's door. Silently, he promised again never to relinquish the great gift Oeta had fostered in him.

Then, Amant smiled. How could he give up music or doubt his worth? The music was him, he was the music; surely he could not stray from himself?

"Never!" he cried, and the sound of his voice bounced back at him from the close-built circle of buildings and from the black stone façade of the Drake's villa. He walked up to the doors. He might as well learn how to perform for the Drake—all young musicians did so, even if their teachers had named them orphics!

3

The Owl's Pocket

LATE in the evening, after the sun had given the sky over to the moon and the rain fell hard on the cobbled streets, Amant found the Owl's Pocket. Tucked up against the Kield wall, with two lighted, diamond-paned windows and a sign nailed over the doorway, it seemed to watch the street humbly, calling little attention to itself. It also looked warm, a good place to rest for awhile. The boy went inside.

The man whom Amant had met earlier hurried to the door. He smiled; his round face was sweaty and his thin hair was laminated to his scalp, as if a painter had granted the man's baldness cover. He seated the boy at a booth before one window. The rest of the room was empty, except for a man who sat at a table in the middle of the place, drinking something that steamed and smelled of cinnamon.

"Raining, still!" said this solitary customer, to no one in particular.

"Ah, yes, indeed," said the owner of the Pocket. He turned to the boy-who-was-thrown-away and said, "Business with the Drake go well for you?"

"No," said Amant. "Not at all."

"Menutti?" called the solitary man. "Menutti, would you come fill this mug again. And we need to settle on this evening's meal, before the rest of them get here."

The owner of the Pocket gave Amant an apologetic shrug and crossed the room to do as he had been asked.

Amant sighed and looked out the diamond-shaped glass at the shop fronts across the street. He watched puddles, stippled by the rain, grow larger and larger from moment to moment. The water reflected the lamps' light in jagged symmetry. When a group of people splashed through one of the greater puddles, their feet shattered the light's patterns. Amant left off watching the water to regard the people. They crossed the puddle and came into the Pocket. Talking and laughing, they crowded into the taverna and seated themselves with the man who had called Menutti away.

Amant turned back to the window and the rain. He felt a little sorry for himself, and he did not wish to listen to the group's noisy pleasantries. Those people had each other for company; he was alone. He had no one, anymore. The family he had hoped to find in Bildron was gone—even the villa of his childhood had been taken from him. There was no place for him in Bildron, nor anywhere.

Bitterly, then, he thought of the Drake. He had spent all afternoon waiting for the ci'esti to listen to his petition. None did. Finally, he had gone away without even a word, angry and tired of sitting in the empty hall, getting stiff and hungry, ignored by the ci'esti as they went about their work, too busy to pay him any mind. By the end of the day, even if they had asked him to sing, he could not have given them anything. The songs had all frozen in his throat. Without speaking to the one ci'esti who had greeted him at the door, he walked out of the twelve-roofed villa and went to the Pocket. At least he might get himself some supper.

The man named Menutti reappeared at the boy's elbow and set a pint of hot, mulled wine down on the table. The boy said, "But . . ."

"You look as if you've been half-frozen. Drink it, and I will bring you a fine supper to match."

"But," said Amant again, "How do you charge for this? You said one-half a linganuli for supper. I only have enough to buy the supper, I fear."

"Well, now, youngster," said Menutti. "Your business left you a little sorry? Say the wine is my treat, since you did not ask after it. Take the drink as a whim of the house and pay for the supper—half a linganuli, as I said."

"Or a song or two," cried out a woman from the group that had shattered the rain-puddles and had joined the solitary man.

Amant glanced past his host to the crowded table of six. There were three women and three men. They all were dressed alike, in pantaloons and ribbons, with blouses of a generous cut, each a different color: black, white, red, green, yellow, and blue.

"Pardon?" said Amant.

The woman laughed and poked the man sitting

next to her. He pushed his chair away from the table and reached down. He sat up with a drum in his hands. Wedging the drum between his legs, he brushed his fingertips over the drumskin and began to tap on it. He started with a simple two beat, tip-tap, tip-tap, but soon it grew into a rhythmic pattering—drum-rain. The laughing woman brushed back her dark curly hair and sang. Amant smiled widely; he knew the song, but he had never heard it made by a jongleur's roundel, as they were about to do.

The song sung that afternoon is called *Port Noma.* If, by chance, you do not know it, it goes this way:

> *Give me a round,*
> *and shackle me down!*
> *Shackle me down!*
> *Shackle me down!*
> *Shackle me down to a bold brave ketch*
> *and take me off to Noma!*
>
> *Take me aground?*
> *No! Shackle me down!*
> *Shackle me down!*
> *Shackle me down!*
> *Shackle me down to a trader's swift,*
> *and off to Noma's market!*
>
> *Pour us a round!*
> *Don't shackle us down!*
> *Shackle us down!*
> *Shackle us down!*
> *Don't shackle us down to a land-locked town,*
> *We're off to the isle of Noma!*

The women's voices took the lower registers and the men sang falsetto, according to the jocular nature of the ballad. They sang it again, and this time Amant walked over and joined in. Singing thus, in a group, lifted his heart.

The drummer ended this second bout with a merry jaunt of improvised pattering, and then the jongleur roundel broke off their song with laughter.

"See, Menutti," said the drummer. "You have found yourself another singer! Now, you must feed the poor boy, for he has sung his heart out, to be sure!"

Amant backed away from the table, shaking his head.

"Come," said the drummer. "Modesty won't do with us. And if you sing again tonight, when the Pocket is full, then perhaps you may be given a free supper, as we are."

Amant shook his head again, glancing at Menutti, expecting disapproval. But the man seemed just as happy as he had been before the impromptu performance, if not more so. He walked over to the drummer and gave the man a light rap on the top of his head, saying, "And who thinks I would feed anyone for such caterwauling! The lot of you can pack yourselves off to the Teka's Eye and do your poor moaning there."

"Shame!" said the dark-haired woman. She smiled as she spoke and shook her fist at Menutti. "Would you be so cruel to us and to this boy with the missive-bird's voice? See, he looks so cold and empty! See how his lips are the same color as the linganuli you want to take from him—blue and cold as your heart, Menutti!"

Amant touched his mouth in surprise and stepped back from the table of jongleurs. Sitting down in the booth his host had given him, he tried to see himself in the glass of the window. *Did he really look as cold as the woman had said? His lips couldn't be that blue!* Yet, he did feel tired. The jongleurs' high spirits embarrassed him; he thought they were mocking him in some way. When the group then ignored him in favor of their supper and their talk, he was relieved. He cupped his hands around the glass mug of wine and stared out the window at the night. It had become so dark that he could no longer see the streets, nor distinguish the buildings from the sky. All he saw was a water-streaked, diaphanous reflection of himself and the blackness. His face seemed almost yellow to him, yellow and sickly and rather too small, lost in all the black night, dwarfed by the candle's blaze that glowed near his elbow.

"You do have a lovely voice," said a woman. Her tone was light and teasing. Amant flinched at the unexpected interruption and found that the jongleur with the dark hair had come over to his table. A small woman, she seemed no older than he, until she tilted her head. Then, the angle of her face and her expression made her youth into age, as if she wore a veil of a younger self and had suddenly taken it off. She asked, "Where are you from?"

"Mossdon Kield."

"Ah, no wonder you sing so pure—did you serve the Ebsters' choir? Yes? O, but did they send you away because you are losing your pretty voice?"

Startled, Amant said, "What?"

She shrugged. "I heard that the Ebsters send young boys away, once their voices change from flute to bass or tenor. You look old enough— indeed, you look older than 'enough'—to trade your missive-bird's voice for a kestrel's croak."

Amant said nothing. He ducked his head behind his mug of wine and sipped the warm liquid to hide his uneasiness. The woman was not altogether wrong. Some youngsters did abandon the Ebsters' Hall when their voices had broken, not because they were sent away, but because they felt embarrassed. Most became chanters with their new voices and, in time, with training, some of those went on to become full Ebsters. But there were always a few who, when the change was done, had no voice left—had, as the woman said, a kestrel's croak. It was a choir youngster's most bitter moment, to know that he could never become a chanter. It was never spoken of lightly, as the jongleur had just done. Amant was angry at her irreverence. And, too, her question about his voice made him uncomfortable; he knew he was old enough for his voice to be changing or have changed. It worried him that it stayed clear and bell-like, that it did not seem to age.

"I know," said the woman suddenly. "You are a chanter! Yes? I should have guessed straightaway, from your manner."

He shook his head, and was about to tell her that he was neither choir-apprentice nor chanter, when she leaned across the table and said, "If you will sing with us tonight, Menutti will feed you for nothing. That is our arrangement with him. A meal for a song. We have kept the Pocket full these past few nights, much to his satisfaction; and he, in turn, has kept us well-fed." She smiled. "Would you sing with us?"

Amant took another sip of his wine before he said, "Why? You sing as a roundel; a seventh would ruin it." He hoped that he sounded as a chanter might: dignified, knowledgeable, and endowed with the good sense not to get involved with jongleurs.

"O, no, not in the ballads, no. Of course we wouldn't take a seventh voice in those. But one of my brothers, Tio—the drummer—he thought you might do a solo for us. He usually takes the solo because we always finish out the night with a lyric. But he isn't up to it this eve, we have had a long, busy day. Would you? A lyric of your own choosing, if you please. We know many lyrics, and if you wish to sing one that we don't know, we learn fast. Come . . . as a chanter, you must be accustomed to performance. We promise you a good audience."

Amant nodded, unwilling to tell the woman the truth—that he had yet to perform for anyone other than his teacher. She had rambled on and flattered him so that he could not bring himself to tell her now that he had been an Ebsters' servant. He smiled what he hoped would look like an indulgent smile and said, "I would be pleased."

She stood up. "And we would be honored. Menutti! Bring another plate, you've another singer to feed." She took the boy by the arm and led him back to the table of jongleurs.

"Tio," she said to the drummer. "Tio, he will

sing for you." She turned to Amant. "What is your name, missive-bird?"

For a moment, the boy-who-was-thrown-away was at a loss. He had told the porter that his name was Nowa, but that his true name was Amant Wuulf-Moas; she did not appear to believe him. So, he would start a new life. Doing so, he should have a new name, one he chose for himself. So he said, "Amant Nowaetnawidef. From Mossdon."

"Amant," said the drummer. "I am Tio Nary, from Kheon, and these are my brothers and sisters, all. Sit and be welcome to the Nary Roundel."

As Amant took the chair he was offered, he asked, "You are all from Kheon? What is it like there?"

"You have never been there?" said Tio.

"No."

"The most beautiful Kield in all the world," said the drummer. "We have a winter home in Kheon, together. In the summer, we travel up to Woodmill and thence to Bildron. We are usually home before now but Menutti has distracted us with his fine suppers."

"They have been helping themselves to my suppers with willing hands," said Menutti. He set a plate before Amant. "To hear Tio, you might think I was forcing them to stay. But, no, they have been stuffing themselves silly and enjoying Bildron!"

At that moment, platters of food, carried by Menutti's two daughters, appeared from the kitchen. There were baked potatoes, sliced seed-cakes, a bowl of corn and beans, a bowl of eels with scallions, and goat cheese, enough for all. The young women set the platters in the center of the table.

Tio laughed. "We are fine jongleurs, the talk of Bildron! The Pocket has never bulged so far. People wait in the streets to buy Menutti's fine suppers."

The host of the Pocket turned his back, as if insulted, and headed off for the kitchen. But he was laughing.

Amant did as his new-found company did— picked out what he wanted, filled his plate, and began to eat. And, as the jongleurs ate, they spoke among themselves of things the boy did not know and of places he had never been. Gradually, he fell to watching them not at all, nor did he listen closely to their talk, but rather he thought about the day. He felt abandoned. He missed Oeta. And yet, the feeling of abandonment was hardly new to him—it had been his shadow-companion all his life and it did not hold the same sort of fear for him as it might have for you or me. He had become the wanderer child, he was the boy-who-was-thrown-away.

But just as the feeling of alone stole into his heart, he remembered that he had not always been so abandoned. When he had lived among the Lo Dianti, in the *dovai*, he had had many *dovai*-brothers and sisters. Indeed, the warm, tightly knit banter of the jongleurs brought memories of similar teasing and talk that he had once shared in the *dovai*. And, as he watched the jongleurs, their faces seemed to blur and shift and melt into the faces of the people of the steppes. He felt as if he had left the Pocket and all his troubles and was back in the Telling Room, tucked in between the eldest of the Lo Dianti children and the littlest, whom he used to hold in his lap. And together, giggling and sighing, sometimes crying, they would listen to the stories of the *dovai*, or stories of wild Aenan and his marvelous powers of change and strength.

Sitting at the jongleurs' table, he let himself drift away from the present into the past; he thought of the *dovai's* music, and of Osei's little voice, as he remembered it, singing to him. Meanwhile, the Pocket grew crowded. Some of the customers stopped when they entered, either to greet Tio or to speak to one of the other singers. As the breaded eels, corn, and beans vanished, so did the silence and the emptiness of the taverna until the one room seemed crammed to the ceiling with the hum of many voices and the intermittent jingling of ceramic or glass. Menutti bustled back and forth from the kitchen to the tables, dispensing food with the aid of his children, both of whom were as round and as full of smiles as their father. Amant woke from his reveries and smiled to think that these people, the family of Menutti, now lived in the brick house that once had been his home. He thought it must be a merry villa, indeed!

Someone tugged at the boy's sleeve. Amant looked around. For a brief moment, he was unnerved by the face he found staring at him. It was only Tio, but somehow his face seemed ugly and menacing—thick eyebrows that grew together over the bridge of his nose, thin lips, and features that seemed over-large for the rest of him. Amant felt himself leaning backward, as if to escape from the face.

Tio smiled (which only made things worse, as far as Amant was concerned) and said, "My sister tells me you are a chanter?"

The boy nodded and glanced away, feeling guilty for his lie and for finding the man's face so repugnant.

"So," continued the jongleur, "you will not mind singing for us *Wild Aenan's Lament*?"

Startled, Amant cleared his throat and tried to keep the surprise from showing. He said, "But . . . that is a sacred song. It . . . it is a choir song and not to be sung lightly. . . ."

"Do you mean to suggest we would play it without skill?"

"N . . . no. But—it is for choir."

"I am not asking you to sing it as a sacred canticle—is that your fear?" The man laughed. "No, no! We don't want any of the Ebsters' power here tonight. Sing it as you would for a child. Surely you have heard it sung lyric, not choral?"

Amant nodded, still troubled. "Once. But . . . it is still difficult."

"Not for a chanter, I would think." Tio frowned. "We play it very well . . . do you doubt me?"

"No, no. . . ."

"Then, you will sing," said Tio. "Yes?"

Amant said nothing. He nodded.

Tio smiled broadly. "Good! Tonight, with your help, we shall be rich!" He stood up and fetched his drum from under the table. The others followed his lead; Tio's brothers On and Ne moved the table to one side while one of the sisters, Rican, moved the chairs into a semicircle that faced the rest of the room. The other two sisters, Ryst and Ietin, set their instruments out: a smaller set of drums, a couple of reed flutes, and a flat, stringed instrument Amant had never seen before.

The boy stood out of the way. He watched Tio warily. For some reason, the drummer had challenged him. *Wild Aenan's Lament* was sacred to the Ebsters, chiefly sung at winter seasonchange to remind the Lake Mother of her grief and so to tell her of their own winter fears. If sung correctly, by the youngest of the choir, with the mature voices of the eldest singing solos at certain intervals, it was said to be terrible and powerful and to have the ability to call the Lake Mother's spirit into the air. Several ancient Ebsters had even claimed to have had a vision of her, in the midst of the song.

Amant had never been permitted to hear the choir give voice to the Lament. Oeta had spoken of it with reverence and awe, enough to make the boy nervous about singing it alone, in a taverna, even as a lyric. He had done it for Oeta, but this was different; the Owl's Pocket was not the Ebsters' Hall. He wondered why the drummer challenged him to this.

The jongleurs took their seats in the semicircle and began the *Port Noma* ballad. Many of the Pocket's diners knew the song and sang along, making the taverna thrum with the sea-pounding percussion of the chanty. As the jongleurs performed, Amant went over the words to *Wild Aenan's Lament* in his head—the descants on the final lines to each phrase were difficult to modulate well.

When *Port Noma* came to an end, there was a moment of silence. Then, Ietin stood up. She smiled to the company and closed her eyes to begin singing a children's song. Perhaps you have heard this song, because it is still sung in the valley Bildron and also, sometimes, in Woodmill Kield. It sounds like this:

> Tĕwĕs pōmĕt, tĕwĕs pōmĕt
> reamànî-tĕs xà nîftĕs.
> Tĕwĕs pōmĕt, tĕwĕs pōmĕt
> ĕnîlĕnànî-tĕs ĕz lîftĕs.
> Tĕwĕs pōmĕt, tĕwĕs pōmĕt
> cheatanî-tĕs ōsoies aües.
> Tĕwĕs pōmĕt, tĕwĕs pōmĕt
> ĕnîlĕnànî-tĕs ĕz aüēs.

Do you recognize it? Perhaps if I show it to you this way; perhaps if I were to write it out, like this:

Do you know this song now? Yes, it is the *Song of the Little Owl!* But the people in the Pocket that night, they would have called it a lullaby without meaning, a nonsense song. Why? Because they did not understand the words. You see, in the long, long ago, Kieldeans were kept ignorant of the first language of Gueame and the Mother's own speech. Many knew that the Lake Mother's tongue existed, but it belonged to the Ebsters and to the Lake Mother's powerful and unknown servitors only. No one else was taught to speak—the Ebsters had forbidden it.

Yet, the first language of the Gueame was not as hidden as the Ebsters supposed. The people of the Tenebrian spoke it; this was the musical language that the boy-who-was-thrown-away heard the night Bildron was burned; this was the tongue he learned as a child in the *dovai*; and these were the words he spoke to the Ebsters when they took him from the slaver's pen. But, you see, they were deaf to what he was saying, because they only knew the words as singers, not as speakers. Too, they thought of Amant as a servant—how would a servant know the Mother's tongue? Impossible! Raiders of the desert spoke gibberish—so did Kieldeans think, in the long, long ago. Thus did Nowaetnawidef keep silent before the Ebsters, even unto Oeta.

That night in the taverna, though, Amant saw that the language had slipped away from the Ebsters' grip in more ways than one. He sat down as the jongleur sang; Ietin sang the lullaby poorly, of course, because she accented none of the words properly and the cadence of each verse was peculiar; she thought she was singing only nonsense sounds, meant to soothe a child to sleep. She sang the *Song of the Little Owl* in the language of the Lake Mother and the tongue of wild Aenan's people, but she did not know it.

Amant sat in the warm, crowded Pocket, listening. Even though Ietin sang the words badly, the song brought him to tears. He sat and heard, and in a few moments, he found himself carried away by the lullaby, as if in a dream. He felt taken from the taverna . . . he was in the *dovai*. It seemed as if he had never left; the pale adobe walls made from the yellow earth of the steppes surrounded him, comforting. And he remembered how, from afar, the warren home seemed more an outcropping of hillocks, which smoked curiously from time to time, rather than a home. How strange it had seemed to him at first! He, a little Kielding boy, a child of the ones-without-shame, accustomed to the villas of Bildron with their stairways and their brick façades! He remembered how, after the raiders had left Bildron Kield to burn, they had ridden long into the night and deep into the forested mountainsides, so far from Amant's villa that the boy knew he was lost forever. He would not be able to find his own way back. He started to cry again as he and the man rode along on the equuilope, but he tried to keep the grief quiet, because he did not want the stranger to know. He thought the man might be angry at such grief. Amant's father had always been angry at tears, as is the custom among the men of Bildron.

The equuilopes moved silently through the rainy dark, up and up and up the mountain. The boy finally fell asleep to the gentle, swift rocking of the animal's stride. When at last he woke from this aching, dreamless slumber, it was daylight. The broad, empty expanse of the steppes stretched around them, everywhere. He had never seen a sky so vast and blue or the sun so brilliant—the light hurt his eyes and made them water. He tried to sit up. He was stiff. His neck hurt when he turned his head. His throat was dry, dry as the dust dancing and swirling around them, thrown in their faces by the wind. He coughed.

The man who held him shifted in the saddle.

He helped the boy to sit straight as he said, "Home, soon."

The boy-who-was-thrown-away looked up at the bearded face that was coated with the yellowish dust and streaked with sweat. He said, "Will you take me home?"

"Home," said the man and pointed to the smoking hillocks in the distance. Then he smiled and said, "My name is Chanutiallin Lo Dianti."

Amant coughed again and said, "Chuntilan Lodayanti?"

Dianti laughed. "ꟿꟿ!" he said, which means something like, 'Ho!'

Amant stared and wondered what he had done wrong.

But the man shook his head at the boy's frightened glance, still laughing. "ꟿꟿ, child, you speak well the language of your people. I knew you were one of Aenan's own!" He gathered the reins in one hand and put his other hand on top of Amant's head. "I give you my name. I give you my family. You are Nowaetnawidef Lo Dianti. ꟿꟿ!! My son."

"Chanter?" said Tio. His voice broke in on Amant's uncanny daydream. The boy blinked and squinted at the drummer, who leaned over and picked up a jug of water beside Amant's feet. "Chanter," he said, "Did you hear my question?"

Amant frowned at the jongleur, who frowned back; so, the boy said, "How can I hear you, over the drums?"

The man shrugged. "You seemed as if you heard nothing, nothing but what was in here." He tapped his head and shrugged again. "Are you ready? We will do one more ballad. Then, you will sing?"

"I will sing," said the boy.

Tio nodded and put the water jug down. The jongleurs began their last ballad, a chanty about an Alentine Isle rebel, while Amant struggled to cast off the memory of the Tenebrian; still, he had become Lo Dianti, even if he had only been a child of the steppes for a short time. His baby-hood in Bildron was something of a dim memory, powerful in its own way, but of the dream-time. It had been the Tenebrian that had truly shaped him. His training at Mossdon, the affection he held for Oeta, and the work he had done as a servant had helped him put aside the *dovai* and become a Kieldean. But now, because he had left Mossdon, his buried past and dreams broke out of their confinement.

He sat in the taverna with his arms folded and tried to listen to the jongleurs. But his heart kept wandering back to the land of the brown and silver-skinned lizards, who baked themselves into a stupor under a summer's sun so fierce it could kill any creature less strong. He belonged to the land of the ringing winds, winds so mighty that they scoured the air clean. And the air had a taste to it besides, a steely taste—iron air. He longed to return to the dry and lonely plains, the desolate and empty steppes that had been the native home of wild Aenan, the place from which he had come to Lake Wyessa, wooing the Lake Mother, the place where Aenan's children lived, scorning the Kieldeans, who knew them not.

Amant smiled to himself. In the Kieldings, wild

Aenan was called a stranger, a wanderer without a home, who had seduced the great Lake Mother of Woodmill. To the Kieldeans, he was—in the long, long ago—unknown, and many thought him dangerous or unworthy of their Mother's great love.

But to the people of the Tenebrian, wild Aenan was a son and a warrior and a father. He had left the desert to seek out the Lake Mother and steal her secrets for his people. She seduced him, bewitched the warrior so that her sibling Death might steal his soul. Yet, she had fallen in love with him and grieved horribly over the wrong she had done him.

As I have said, in the long, long ago, people were ignorant. Before the making of Amant Wuulf-Moas' greatest songs, before his wisdom helped to give birth to the Reconciliation and joined the Tales of Kheon with the *Haaimikin Oide*, no one knew where the truth lay; even now, who can say if Amant has woven for us the truth behind wild Aenan's love for the Lake Mother or the truth behind the Lake Mother's love for wild Aenan? Who can say the truth behind any love? The Tenebrian people who remain are little seen; the ways of the Kieldings have changed; and the boy-who-was-thrown-away is no longer a boy, nor even a man, but a memory and a ghost. Only the songs and the tales and their magic remain. But if you are a dreamer, as I, perhaps the truth is not as important as the wonder of the music and the magic.

However, in the Pocket on that night of the jongleurs, Amant was not concerned with the future and what you and I might believe. He was too busy thinking of how he might sing *Wild Aenan's Lament*. He rubbed his face with both hands, to wake himself from the memories of the Tenebrian and prepare for the song.

The jongleurs ended the ballad with a flourish. Tio touched the boy's shoulder, and Amant stood, as he knew a soloist must. He walked to the center of the jongleurs' semicircle. Rican stood and bowed to him. He bowed in return, seeing by her movement that she was to lead off the solo. She picked up a flute. When she introduced the Lament, Amant heard a surprised murmur in the taverna. Quickly, the whole room quieted, awaiting the song. At first, the hush frightened the boy. Then, he felt a surge of joy: They were here to listen to him, and he was there to sing! He was a chanter! If the Drake would not give him audience, what did it matter? He had an audience, here, in the taverna.

The drum's chorus began behind him, weaving in the percussion of the sad lyric as Rican sounded her flute. Amant closed his eyes and began:

> *O, where have you gone,*
> *my own beloved?*
> *Have you followed your sister*
> *gone back to the Sea?*
> *O, I have not left you,*
> *my own beloved.*
> *I have not followed my sister,*
> *nor gone back to the Sea.*
>
> *O, where have you gone,*
> *my own beloved?*

I have sought you among the bamboo,
I have sought you by the Sea.
O, I have not left you,
my own beloved.
I am here, in our home;
it is you who have gone.

O, where have I gone,
my own beloved?
Have I followed your sister,
down to the Sea?
O, yes, you have gone,
my own beloved,
down to the Sea's shore
where no tree grows.

As Amant sang the long, sad phrases, he felt his heart once again leave the Pocket as he sailed off on the dark sea of memory. The grief of the music spoke to the grief he felt for his mother, who was now a gate-porter, old and gray and confused; for his father, Lent, who had buried a stranger as his own son; for the Tenebrian people, his adopted father, Chanutiallin Lo Dianti, who died under the corsair's blade, his adopted mother left to die on the bitter, winter steppes. The grief carried him deeply inside himself and far away from the taverna to a place where he saw, for an instant, all the loss that simple living bears—all the partings and all the changes and all the deaths that each of us must suffer. And the sorrow of these would go on and the changes would go on, until he too died and must go to the

Sea of Sansel's Net where the spirit might, perhaps, find peace someday.

Seeing this for the first time was too much for
him, too much to accept. The sorrowful, lilting
phrases of the lyric kept the clarity of the losses he
must face vivid to him, until he had to flee. He let
his heart flee back into the past, away from this
place of loss and changes and death. Again, he
fled back to the *dovai*, where he found his *dovai*-
mother waiting for him. She was warm, and her
lap was ample. He could almost hear the sweet-
ness of her voice. Indeed, he brought that sweet-
ness out from his memory and into the sad cadences
of the lyric he was singing, as he remembered the
way she had sung the lullaby of the Little Owl. He
put her heart into his singing; he put himself into
his *dovai*-mother's heart and, suddenly, he found
that he spoke *Wild Aenan's Lament* in the Mother's
tongue:

$$\mathcal{9} \sim \mathcal{v} \mathcal{9} (\mathcal{1} \mathcal{7} \sim (\mathcal{1}) \sim \mathcal{6} \mathcal{7} \sim \mathcal{6} \vee \mathcal{7} \mathcal{6} \mathcal{7} (\mathcal{6} \sim$$
$$\mathcal{6} \sim \mathcal{9} \mathfrak{c} \mathcal{v} (\mathcal{1}) \mathfrak{c}$$

> . . . *Hêh, lōĕdĕn-sĕn kōnōanî*
> *mîhearda.* . . .

Then, something . . . odd . . . happened. He
felt as if he were no longer entirely . . . himself.
The shape of his face felt as if it were changing, as
if it were reforming, growing older and broader.
His skin tingled and crawled; his limbs felt weak, a
sort of watery, melting sensation . . . and he knew
what was happening. It was the power of wild
Aenan in him, part of his being *dowanaten*. It had

happened to him twice before—once, as a child in Bildron, when he wished to become a puppy on that night he-had-been-thrown-away, and once when he had gone with the raiders of the *dovai*, to corral equuilope. He was becoming his *dovai*-mother; he was changing into her and if he did not stop the *dowanaten* he would become his stepmother!

Amant caught his breath, in a panic. He cut off the song, too quickly for the jongleurs. They continued to play, expecting him to finish out the line. Someone cried a wordless gasp of surprise. Amant bolted from the taverna, grateful that the room was rather dark and that he had been standing so near the door.

Outside, the cold made him shake. The rain pricked his skin with little jabs of ice. But he took a deep breath and let the cold inside him, to clean out the taste of the *dowanaten* and to chase away the memory of loss that grief had brought to him. He ran down the street to escape the music and the mourning and the haunted power of wild Aenan that lurked inside him.

4

The Teka

THE RAIN thinned to a mist. Fog clotted the night air, turning the darkness to a gray twilight wherever the street lights shone. Amant ran over the cobblestones, past the shop fronts, past the silent homes. He ran at an easy pace, neither hectic nor slow. He knew, or thought he knew, which streets would take him back to the porter's lodge, and so he kept running, despite the fog. He was sure that he would soon find the lodge and be far away from the Owl's Pocket, the jongleurs, and the memories he had called up. As he ran, the power of Aenan that had gripped him lessened its hold, until he was entirely himself again. He took a deep breath; he hoped that no one in the taverna had truly seen the *dowanaten*. He hoped the whole matter would be passed off as a trick of the lamplight, or the wine and the late hour.

He ran and kept on running. The fog grew denser. It was not long, however, before he suspected he was lost. He slowed his loping gait to a walk and looked at the villas as he went along.

Here, a stoop poked out of the swirling fog; there, a painted doorway; here, a lattice fence; there, an ironwork trellis. He stopped before a red door and wondered where he was. How far had he strayed from the main road? Where was the Owl's Pocket? The porter's lodge? How far had he to go? He peered into the haze, hoping to discern at least the Kield wall. He turned around, slowly, in a circle. If he could find the wall, he could follow it. Eventually it would lead him round to the gates.

But, even the wall had been eaten by the grayness. He could not see anything besides the red door and the wet pavement at his feet. He stepped closer to the door. "Should I knock?" he asked himself. He was shivering, and the mist felt as if it were working its slow way through every layer of his wool and homespun clothing, to wet his skin and steal his warmth. Despite the late hour, despite his reluctance to speak with strangers, Amant rapped on the door and stepped aside. The door opened. But it opened only a little, only a crack. He waited for someone to speak. He was met by silence. The door had no keeper. He pushed on it and it swung inward. Darkness. Then, a rank urine odor escaped, along with a foul air of moldy desertion and dusty disuse. He coughed, turned away, and walked back into the empty street.

What should I do? he wondered. He looked around again, hoping that the fog would thin. If nothing else, eventually the sun would rise and bring him light . . . but he would be exhausted! He was exhausted already. He took an uncertain step and then stumbled over something that yelped and whined. Amant regained his balance and squinted.

At his feet sat . . . what? A puppy? A miserable, wet creature, black and scarcely larger than a man's fist. It was staring up at him, he who must seem a giant to such a small thing, a giant with clumsy, hurtful feet. Its eyes shown green, and it bared its puppy teeth to the monster that had stepped on its tail. Amant glanced at the open, red door. The puppy must have come from the foul little room. Although the creature growled at him, it was so tiny, just a black spot of fur and teeth, that he laughed. This laughter seemed to work some change on the creature, because it stood and launched itself at Amant's foot, worrying the toe of his boot with its teeth. In a moment, it found the boy's trouser and promptly bit his calf.

Amant leaned down and gave the puppy's rump a sound swat. The creature yelped again and left off its biting. The boy started to walk away, intent upon finding the wall before he was too cold to move. He tried to ignore the fact that his calf smarted from the puppy's attack.

The creature followed him. It got itself tangled up between his feet again and got its tail pinched under a heel. So, finally, Amant stooped and picked up the persistent thing by the scruff, careful to keep his hands away from the teeth.

On closer inspection, the boy decided that the puppy was a very ugly little thing, and perhaps because it was so ill-formed it had been left in the room to die. It was all rib cage and chest, with the knobs of its shoulders sticking up high from its back, two bony joints covered too thinly with fur. Its front paws were clawed more sharply than he had expected; it had a long, pointed snout and floppy ears. Both snout and ears were large for its head. It snapped its jaws at the boy as he examined his treasure; then, it started to cry in a peculiar high-pitched manner, a thinner, reedier sound than Amant had ever heard a puppy make. It was such a pitiful, painful cry that the boy scooped the creature into one arm and stroked its head with his free hand. The puppy closed its eyes.

For a moment, Amant thought perhaps he ought to leave the animal in the room from whence it came. What was he going to do with it otherwise? But the abandoned villa was so rank and chilly; whoever had left the puppy there had surely meant for it to die. He could not do such a thing; so he tucked the puppy closer to him and groped his way through the fog, with a little black spot of fur making a pouch of warmth against his stomach.

The night, so quiet, so cold and wet, seemed to mock his efforts to orient himself. He wandered. The Kield wall seemed to have vanished altogether, along with any landmarks. His legs and feet began to cramp. He kept flexing his hands to keep them from going numb. He had spent the whole of that afternoon in the damp hall of the Drake Villae's home, alone, unnoticed and freezing. Was he to spend the whole of the night freezing too? Would he get a sore throat that would make his voice sound like broken glass? Wouldn't that be a fine thing for a chanter who wished to join the Academe!

He stopped walking and stood still. He was so frustrated he was close to either a scream or tears. How could the Drake and her ci'esti simply ignore him? How would he ever join the Academe, if he couldn't even get an audience with the Drake in

Bildron? He closed his eyes and sighed, then tucked one hand under the puppy, and began to walk again. But now, he let his body walk him. He did not try to see through the mist. He did not try to orient himself. He simply walked. He listened to the echoes of his footsteps against the wet pavement and tasted the iron of the cold air. He stroked the puppy's fur; he could feel the small heart beat against the palm of his hand where he held the creature. Eventually, he was calm enough to chide himself for his haste in leaving the Pocket; he decided that should he remain lost until dawn, it was his own fault. He had panicked.

By the Mother's granting, he thought, *I will learn a lesson in patience tonight!* And then he laughed silently because he could almost hear Oeta speaking those very same words to him one afternoon. The Ebster, annoyed that his pupil could not sit still for his lesson, had made the boy play scales until the pads of his fingers were so sore that the following afternoon, he could hardly bear to even look at the viola.

Amant kept walking, more to keep warm than to get anywhere. He thought about Oeta as he went along; then, he began to think about Osei. She had loved the milky evening fogs of Bildron. She would sit at the window of their bedroom at night, hours after the last adult had dropped off to sleep. The only sounds were the sighs and settlings of the house and perhaps a mouse or two. Amant remembered waking to find a single candle's light disrupting the midnight gloom; there she would be, all wrapped in her pink-flowered blanket, her dark hair a tangle and her pale brown eyes wide as she stared out the window glass, watching the fog twist and curl. Once, she told Amant that she had made friends with the fog. She said it came to wake her up and tell her stories with its patterns. Amant secretly thought she was dreaming as she sat up to watch the night fog, because he often found her asleep the next morning, with her forehead against the glass. He told her that fog could not tell tales; that she had been dreaming. Her only answer was a smile.

Remembering his sister-cousin, Amant felt his throat grow tight—and his heart, too. He had to find her. Wherever she had gone, wherever her mother had taken her, Amant knew he had to try to find her. He would. He promised himself and her dream-ghost that he would.

He looked up. Was that a light he saw? He blinked and cocked his head in surprise. Like a single star set in an overcast sky, hazy and haloed by the moisture, yet still strong enough to show itself, he saw a yellow daub of light. It seemed suspended in mid-air, all alone. He headed toward it, as a swimmer in a murky sea; the closer he got, the brighter it shone until it illuminated a window, then, a windowsill, a stone wall, a door—the porter's lodge. The porter had left a lamp burning for him. The door was unlocked. He went inside, blew out the light, and crept off to bed, taking the puppy with him.

☆

A KNOCK on the bedroom door woke him the next morning. Unsure of where he was and befuddled by too few hours of sleep, he mumbled, "Oeta?"

The porter did not open the door. Through it, she said, "Your carrier comes soon. Would you eat before you leave?"

Amant pushed himself up onto his elbows. "Please," he said, his confusion gone. "I would." He turned over onto his back and his feet brushed against a warm and heavy dollop of puppy at the bottom of the pallet. He sat, staring at the animal. He did not wish to get out of bed. The blanket was warm; the sheets smelled of him, of his hair, of his skin—a comfortable nest. He did not know where he would be on the coming eve, and so he did not want to move from the comfort he now enjoyed. He could not even conjure up a fanciful picture of the Academe, for solace. Every thought he framed split and vanished and left him with only apprehension.

He yawned and stretched, prodding the puppy with his toes. The animal shivered and then lifted its head . . . and Amant saw that what he had rescued from the fog was not much like a puppy at all. What exactly he had found, he could not say immediately. He watched it stand up on its four legs and stretch itself out. It was a black-furred creature with a thick roll of dense, gray fur around its neck and head. It had a dog's long snout and eyes that were not round, but oblong and narrow and black, with specks of gold, giving the creature's face a quality wholly unlike any dog the boy had ever seen.

What was it? As slowly as he possibly could, the boy got off the bed. He tensed with discovery as it came to him what he had found, although he hoped he was mistaken. Yet, when he saw that the points he had taken for bony shoulder blades were, in fact, the points of wings—leathery wings, folded up tight and flat against the creature's back, nearly hidden by the thick fur—Amant believed, despite all legend and logic, that he had found a teka.

In our times, now that the tekas are plentiful and mighty once again, it is hard to remember that in the long, long ago there were so few. When my great-great-grandfather was a boy, to see one flash across the sky, flying to its eyrie, was rare. So, for Amant to think that he had found a teka was a startling thing, indeed.

The teka-who-was-not-a-puppy began to lick itself, smoothing down its fur and biting itself with its sharp teeth. It spread its wings, to reach a spot. Amant jumped back a little, surprised by the length of the leathery span. The wings were much larger than he had supposed. Their webbing was a translucent pink near the ends, but mostly they were brown and blue-veined with a bursting mass of minuscule vein lines, like a new, spring leaf—soft, delicate, but sturdy.

Carefully, Amant sat back down on the bed, to see if the animal would come to him. It stared at the intruder of its bath with a glance that suggested the question, "how dare you?" The boy giggled and tried to stroke the small head. Ducking, the teka dodged the hand but then, capriciously, it lifted its nose to sniff at the fingertips. It licked one finger, sniffed again, and allowed itself to be petted.

Amant finally mustered the courage to pick up the teka and put it in his lap. It stayed there, curled against his stomach, while he examined . . .

her. Enduring the poking, the teka only snapped at him once, when he attempted to spread a wing. He snatched his hand back, away from the nipping teeth, and said, "You're an anxious thing!" He shook his head. "Where did you come from?"

The sound of his voice and the shake of his head startled the teka. She fairly leaped from his lap back to the bed with her wings spread and flapping. They sounded like shoe soles, slapping against pavement. The teka pranced about, her tiny tail pointed at the ceiling.

"How did you come to be in that room?" he asked the animal, as if she might answer him. "There are no tekas left in Gueame. I mean . . . the tekas all died . . . didn't they?" He stared at the animal. She stared back at him, then folded up her wings and sat.

"I thought," said the boy, "that all the tekas had died. . . ."

The porter knocked at the door again, scaring both the boy and the animal.

Annoyed, Amant said, "I'm coming!" But even as the words were spoken, he caught his breath. The tone of his voice was unfit for a guest. He sounded, even to himself, like a petulant child answering his mother.

There was no reply from the other side of the door.

Amant scrambled to his feet and dressed. The teka ignored him as he stuffed his belongings into his satchel. Instead, she jumped to the floor and began to chase her tail, rolling upon her back, and making little, ineffective leaps at the ever-elusive quarry.

As Amant worked to tidy the room and collect his things, he pictured to himself the frieze that had been painted on the walls in Oeta's chambers. The frieze was a version in miniature of the full-wall frescoes in the room where the Ebsters gathered to sing each equinox for the pleasure of the Drake of Mossdon. The frescoes depicted the final valley war, when the Drake who was named Quedahl settled the disputes between her thirteen children and thus brought peace to Gueame.

Shall I tell you that story? Amant had heard it told in this same way many a time at Oeta's knee because it was the Ebsters' own favorite out of all the Tales of Kheon. It goes this way:

In the days of long, long ago, there was once a powerful Drake. Her name was Quedahl. She was beloved of many men. To each she bore a child, and so, in the course of her young life, she had thirteen children. Her children grew strong and beautiful, almost as beautiful as she was, and as different from one another as their human fathers had been. But, they were terrible in their jealousy of one another. They were always fighting. As they grew older, their fighting became worse, until they had made a shambles of their mother's villa in Mossdon.

Quedahl grew impatient with her offspring and their bickering. So, she went out into the land of Gueame, and visited with her sisters and brothers and cousins in all the thirteen Kields: the Western Kields—Senon, Laet, Kheon, Nathin; the Northern Kields—Pacot, Bildron, Marridon; the Southern Kields—Woodmill, Cutoe,

Athet, Adeo; and the Eastern Kields—Mossdon, Lethin, and Nost. To each of her relatives she put the same question: "Will you take one of my children, to live with you for a seasonchange or two?"

And, of course, they agreed. No one could ever say "nay" to Quedahl. She was the youngest of them and much favored.

So, to the thirteen Kields of Gueame came the thirteen children of Quedahl, each of them still as jealous of the others as ever. Within one single turn of harvest to planting, they were battling again. But now their fighting had gone from the childhood villa, where weapons had been shoes or pillows or maybe crockery but nothing more serious than these, to warring with words and wishes. They gathered to them each a small band of followers— who had listened to the words and believed that the Lake Mother would grant the wishes.

And so, whenever one band would meet another, they would skirmish, as dogs after the same morsel of food. These battles, some of them small and some terrible, were later called the Valley Wars.

And the harvests were not made in Adeo, where luscious fruit rotted, falling from its trees untouched; the harvests were not made in Woodmill, where the corn was eaten by straying cattle and the goats roamed free from the goatherd; cloth was not spun in Nost, where the sheep were not pastured well and were easy prey for the mountain wolves; in Laet, the tailors were all busy making battle clothes, quilted trousers, and quilted jackets to protect the foolish fighters from one another's attacks.

Worst of all, the children of Quedahl trained their tekas to battle.

Now, as we have seen, the teka is an odd creature, with black fur and leathery wings, a cousin to the little night bats that you can find in the caves of Mount Oron, or in the foothills of Brustai. But they are not bats, although the appearance is somewhat the same and both prefer the night to day. They are wiser than bats, sharper than birds, and, like the eagle with its mate, they are utterly loyal; if the teka consents to be companion to a person, it is as loyal to that person as it is to its mate. How this came about, the Tales of Kheon do not explain. The *Haaimikin Oide* claims that wild Aenan taught the animal loyalty, when he wanted a companion to trust as he went out upon his search for the child whom Death had stolen from him and the Lake Mother. Amant Wuulf-Moas has made a song of the teka who was wild Aenan's companion; but that happened long after the Valley Wars, during the Reconciliation.

Now, in times of peace in the long, long ago, the Tales of Kheon say that the tekas were trained only to hunt—to fly off the ground on command and catch birds or other sorts of prey for food. But when the children of Quedahl began to bicker and sow ill will, they taught their tekas to go out into the night, hunting people.

The Kields grew to fear the cry of the teka, that fierce and awful "keir-ah" of the night-ones come flying over the hillsides to do some dire bidding. Many a person died under their claws. So it was that the teka's cry came to be known as Death's

Clarion, a beckoning call summoning souls to the Shore of Sansel's Net.

When Quedahl saw what her children had done, she was angry. She had thought that sending them away from home, putting them under the tutelage of her family, and separating them from one another would teach her wildlings some discipline. Instead, her sisters and cousins and brothers had gone lazy and did not truly care much for their foster brats. They had not paid them mind, as they should have. Now they appealed to Quedahl for help, saying that as a mother, it was her duty to punish her children. And it is told that, secretly, the rulers of the thirteen Kields were glad to admonish Quedahl for her wildlings' behavior, because they feared her offspring might supplant their own. A sound fear, as it has come to pass!

Quedahl went out from her home in Mossdon, disguised as a poor chanter. She made her way to the Lake Mother's secret island villa in Woodmill.

It is said that Trost, the Lake Mother, did favor young Quedahl; it is said, further, that the servitors of Trost, who greeted the Drake when she knocked on their door, treated her with deference. As for the rest, who can know? Did Quedahl speak with the Lake Mother herself? Did she, indeed, meet wild Aenan and the little child with no name? Perhaps she was permitted such a great honor. What the Tales do tell is that Quedahl spoke her wish at the Lake Mother's wishing stone and that the wish was this—that she might teach each of her children the true meaning of love.

And so it was that Quedahl was granted

thirteen fabulous powers, as told in the Thirteen Tales of Mossdon's Drake. Each power was particular to each wildling, so that Quedahl might teach all of her children the meaning of love differently, in a way each would best understand.

I might tell you all Thirteen Tales someday, if you have the patience, but here I will tell you only of the tekas and what became of them. Quedahl loved her children, yet her anger with them was just as strong. And so, because she had given all her mercy to her children, she had none for the tekas. It was upon these creatures that she spent her great fury. She took them from her wildlings, over cries and lamentations, and she chained them together with a linkage of gold. She led them off to the White Sea, to be drowned. This is what the frieze on Ebster Oeta's wall showed—the drowning of the tekas and the end of the Valley Wars. It is a favorite subject with painters, and it appears in many a Drake's villa to remind them that their ancestor Quedahl brought peace to Gueame.

Adjusting the clasp of his coat, Amant stared down at the black ball of fur roving about on the bedroom floor. She hardly seemed vicious. What was he to do with her? He frowned, wondering if he should take her to the Drake of Bildron. But would the Drake, following the precept of her ancestor, drown the teka? Was this the reason she had been left to starve or freeze in that stinking little room?

Amant crouched and held out his hand to the animal. She stopped chasing her tail and looked at him, the ruff of fur around her neck rising. Then, suddenly, she pounced, wings outspread, claws retracted, to land in his arms. He rubbed her head and decided that he could not let her be drowned or starved. He would take her with him, and, once the carrier had gone away from Bildron Kield into the countryside, he would let her go.

He grasped the creature by the scruff and put her in his coat's cowl. She fumbled around in the folds of the hood for a few moments, nearly choking him. He held the clasp at his neck until the teka settled down. Once she did, she clung to his back through the cloth with all four claws but did not scratch him. He waited a few minutes, to see if she would stay where he had put her. Then, satisfied that the creature was hidden for the time being, he left the room.

The porter had set a bowl of doughy gruel and a sweet bun on a tray beside the hearth for him. He sat and began to eat; tearing the sweet roll into bits, he fed the teka small morsels. He did not know what tekas usually ate, though he suspected mice or grasshoppers or infant birds might be more welcome than bread. But the tiny thing in his cowl seemed content to take what she was offered.

He heard the porter close her bedroom door and walk up the hall toward him. She set a kettle over the flame and sat down across from him, as they had sat together a night before. She folded her hands in her lap and said, "I went out there, yester eve."

"Out there?"

She nodded.

"Out where?" he asked.

But she did not answer.

Puzzled, the boy ate the handful of cereal left in

his bowl and licked his fingers clean. As he put the empty bowl on the tray, he said, "Can you tell me—where is Osei?" He tried to ask the porter-who-was-his-mother this question calmly, naturally, as if he were asking after the time of the carrier's arrival, or some other such plain, day-to-day fact.

The porter frowned. "Osei went with Giolla. Poor thing!"

"And where? Where did they go?"

The porter unfolded her hands and rubbed them together. Then she let them fall back into her lap. She said, "Giolla would go to Kheon. Her lover was there, Osei's father. Poor little child. She could not understand where her 'brother' had gone. She used to stand on the stoop in those afternoons before Lent died, waiting for my boy to come home. I told her he would never come, that he had gone to the Sea of Sansel's Net, but Osei did not believe me. She kept waiting. She said that she dreamed of my son and that he was with wild Aenan." The porter gave a short laugh. "I knew he was with wild Aenan! In the Sea, as Death willed it. Did I tell you, I went out there yester eve? To the alder trees, where I buried them." She stood up and glanced at the boy-who-was-thrown-away and she said, "Osei always knew that you would come home, one day."

Amant held his breath. Slowly, he let it out and said, "Mother?"

The porter glanced away. She did not answer him. After another moment, she took the steaming kettle off the flame and said, "The carrier comes. I hear it. Go and see."

Amant did not move. He said, "Seftenir?"

"Go and see," she replied, as she poured water into a teapot.

He stood and strode over to the door that led outside the Kield walls. He yanked the door open and found that the porter had been right—the carrier stood on the road. It was an old carrier, the bright yellow paint peeling from its sides and the canvas covering patched. The donkey team looked tired and thin. Two passengers climbed out of the covered wagon. They stretched. The driver busied himself by hooking up the team's feed bags.

The porter walked out of the lodge. She carried three mugs of tea on a tray and gave one each to the three newcomers. When she handed the driver the last mug, she stopped to speak with him.

Amant turned from the door and went back inside to the warm room, the snug hearth, the chairs pulled up close to the fire, and the aromatic herb bunches at the mantel. He did not want to leave the mother whom he had found. Still, he thought that she wished him to go away—nothing she said or did showed she wanted him to stay. He decided that too much time had passed. There was no place for him in the porter's lodge or in the porter's life. He stared at the floor, seeing nothing and feeling as if he were no one, a ghost.

Finally, in a haze of emptiness, he walked back down the hall to the weaving room where he had left his belongings. The satchel sat where he had propped it up beside the pallet. On top of the sack, he saw two small bundles. He looked closer: A seed-cake wrapped in a colored cloth was the first bundle; the second was a soft bag with a frayed cord and it held his violin. He sat down next to the pallet and cried.

5
To the Cape

THE LOW white winter sun made the tree shadows long and thin; it made Amant's shadow long and thin too, as he paced up and down in the field, trying to warm himself. He stretched his sore muscles and his skinny shadow stretched with him. He was stiff from sitting on the carrier's hard bench. His back ached, as if he were an old man in a rainstorm.

The carrier was empty. The driver, having pulled to the side of the road to let the donkeys graze, had fallen asleep. The other two passengers, whose names Amant still did not know, even after a full day's travel, had disappeared into the nearby grove.

Late autumn crickets gave their music to the boy. He sat down beside the abandoned carrier to listen. He wished he had a blanket; the air was nippy and promised another cold night. Across the field, a flock of blue crowns rose from the branches of a barren alder and rode the breeze in a blue ribbon. They made no sound; the fluid line of their flight was noted by a red crown, which called out its sweeping cry. The call was answered by another's, then another's; finally a third, the sound getting ever more distant.

The teka in Amant's hood stirred at the echo of the red crowns' cries. She crawled up from the bottom of the hood and, before the boy could move, she leaped from his shoulder to the air. Amant got to his feet and chased after the teka as she soared across to the alder. He shouted. In return, she made the cry that he had heard spoken of in the Tales—"keir-ah!" He ran, as she soared again and glided silently in circles around the tree. He watched and as he watched, he suddenly wished that he too might soar. He wished he might join her flight, angling on the wind and drifting smoothly in a perfect loop.

Amant ran. He felt the wind against his body; he held out his arms. Faster and faster did he go, following the teka, trying to catch up with her as she sped along the edge of the grove. The boy laughed with the sheer pleasure of running; his legs pumped and his feet seemed to have eyes, so nimbly did he dash across the field without tripping. The wind made his ears burn, brushed through his hair, and he laughed again—but the laughter came out as "keir-ah!" and in the next instant, he had launched himself into the air! He was no longer a boy; he was airborne, a teka, as fiery as any wild-spawn. His shoulders had sprouted wings, his hair had turned to fur. . . .

Then, as suddenly as it had come to him, the power of Aenan went, and the boy found himself lying on his back in the field grass, staring up at the empty white sky. He flexed his fingers; he flexed his toes. He licked his dry lips, caught his breath, and sat up. He was not a teka. He was Amant.

"Amant," he whispered, to reassure himself. Shaking, sweating despite the cold, he took several deep breaths to slow his heart. He buried his hands under his arms, so that he would not have to see how unsteady they were. When he pushed himself to his feet, his calves tingled, and he had some trouble keeping his balance.

He felt ill, standing there alone. The teka landed at his feet, but he shied away from it, afraid.

"Dowanaten," he whispered to himself. "Again!" Twice in so few days the gift of wild Aenan had come swift upon him! He started, slowly, to walk back toward the barren alder and the carrier. He remembered that dawn when his *dovai*-father, Lo Dianti, had found him writhing in the desert soil changing into one of the banes of the steppes, a sky-painted coiler.

It had happened in this way: A party of seven raiders had gone out one summer morn to corral equuilopes. For the warriors, this was sport as well as a task, and they were full of cheer as they made camp. The wild flock had been spotted to the south; in the afternoon the warriors would set out after it.

This was Nowaetnawidef's first corral; he was tense with excitement and with his desire to do well before his *dovai*-father. He had risen before the sun, as Lo Dianti asked, to saddle their mounts. He crept past the sleeping raiders, pausing only to feed the fire, which had burned low. The flames rose, shadowing the others and the slumbering equuilopes curled up on the rough turf. He stepped over his father and knelt to Lo Dianti's mount. The creature lifted its squat, broad muzzle off the ground and nudged the boy, nearly knocking him over. Nowaetnawidef twined his fingers in the beast's curly coat and laid his chin on the equuilope's shoulder. A rough tongue and velvety lips began to explore the boy's head. He giggled, and looked out across the empty steppes toward the far-off peaks that were the foothills of Mt. Oron.

The sky-painted coiler spat and lifted its knife-edged head not a foot in front of the boy and the equuilope. The equuilope quivered and bolted to its feet, knocking Nowaetnawidef backward. The boy scrambled to his knees and leaped toward a clump of brush.

The sky-painted coiler spat again. It had backed off when the equuilope had moved, but now it crawled forward on its four stubby legs. Its long, smooth tail undulated. The boy found himself staring at the slender head and the sky-blue stripes on the thing's back and briefly saw himself dead, his throat torn open by the coiler's claws. He glanced around once. There was no place to hide, and if he ran, the coiler would merely follow, for despite its awkward-looking body, a coiler can move like the wind. The Tenebrians called it the bane of the earth because of its speed and because it had a tenacity beyond any other creature. Once it scented its prey, it would not relinquish the chase until the prey was caught.

The boy knew this; only last season had his kith lost a child younger than he to the coiler's speed. And so, as was the custom among the desert people, he began to sing to wild Aenan, to ask for a swift dying. And the part of Nowaetnawidef that was Amant also wished to the Lake Mother, asking for the solace of her embrace when his soul began its journey to the Shore of Sansel's Net.

The sound of his own voice bolstered his courage. And, strangely, the coiler did not move in on its prey. Nowaetnawidef stared at the creature and then ... the earth slipped out from under him. Had he fallen? Was the coiler at his neck? No ... he thrashed about, trying to stand but his arms and legs would not hold him, they had shrunk and all over his body he felt a crawling, as if he were shedding his skin the way a snake might.

"(?(?!" cried a man, as if from a great distance. The voice jolted the boy, and he instinctively ducked, rolling himself into a ball, as a keen lance whiffled past him and pinned the coiler to the earth.

He sat. He was able to stand. His legs and arms tingled, but they were not shrunken. He touched the skin of his arm and saw that it was whole, and then he looked at the coiler. It was dead, its thin, black blood staining the yellow earth.

Lo Dianti stepped up to the coiler and pulled out his lance. He said, without looking at the boy, "I heard your song."

Nowaetnawidef nodded. He said, "I believed it was my time." He hoped he sounded brave.

The warrior lifted the dead creature by its tail, and looked at his adopted son. "Wild Aenan guided my throw, child ... for there were two coilers here, not a moment ago."

"Two?" The boy shot a glance behind him, and

then he understood. He said, "Me?" He sat down as if his legs had collapsed.

Lo Dianti flung the coiler onto the earth near his saddle bags and crouched next to Nowaetna-widef. For a few moments, they sat in silence. Then, the boy said, "No."

Lo Dianti shrugged and put on his riding gloves. "You are *dowanaten*. You are haunted."

"In dreams," said the boy. "Those are just dreams."

"Dreams take form, if you are haunted. As it was with wild Aenan. A gift to you, to tell you that you belong to the kith, truly." He stood up, and pointed to where the frightened equuilope had bounded. The creature was now grazing on the bunch grass, unconcerned. "Come and help me saddle her," he said.

The boy stood, too. He asked, "What do I do with the gift?"

Lo Dianti shook his head. "That is not for me to tell you. We will speak with the orphics and with your uncle Mathisianii after the corral. For now, be well, my son! Aenan favors you. In time, you will learn to carry the power with grace. But come, we have a flock to chase."

Amant leaned against the trunk of the alder and whispered to the memory of his *dovai*-father, "But there was no time to learn from Mathisi-anii. . . ." He gazed across the field at the carrier and wondered if the driver had waked yet—it would be good to leave.

"Keir-ah!" cried the teka.

Amant looked toward the sound. The animal was sitting in the top branches of the tree overhead. Then, she sprang into the air again. Within a few moments, she was lost to sight.

He stared after the creature, half-hoping she would return and half-hoping she would not. He waited until the white sun had gone from the sky, dusking the light and making the air cooler. When the teka did not appear, he walked back to the carrier with his hands in his pockets and his heart calmed. He had decided what he must do: he must find a wishing stone and ask that the Lake Mother take away the power that wild Aenan had granted him. Why? Because, he told himself, he could never learn to be *dowanaten*, now that the *dovai* had died. Of what use would the gift be among the Kieldeans, who feared such a power? The one time he had dared question Oeta about it, he had been told that the 'insight,' as the Kieldeans called it, was a curse to any who were not trained as an Ebster. Only the Ebsters—and the unknown, invisible servitors of the Lake Mother who lived with her in her hidden villa of Lake Wyessa—knew how to use the insight. At first, Amant had tried to argue with Oeta about being *dowanaten*; but the old man had rebuked his servant sharply, seeing his tale as an impious raider's boast.

Amant kicked a stone and sent it skittering across the grass. He clasped his hands behind his back and told himself that the teka's disappearance was for the best. Had he not been about to set it free that night? He nodded. All was well. He would reach Kheon and find the Academe and study music, and he would try to forget the *dovai* altogether. He kicked another stone; one of the donkeys brayed, but the driver slept on. The couple had not yet returned. Amant climbed into the carrier and fetched his viola.

He sat down in the matted grass beside the tall, spoked carrier wheel and warmed his fingers as best he could before tuning the strings. The crickets, which had stopped chirping when he had intruded upon their grass, now resumed their own song. Amant set his bow to the strings. He considered for a moment, then he chose to play part of the dirge he had composed, based on the theme of *Wild Aenan's Lament.* The brief dirge, to be sung by two voices if possible, had been an exercise of Oeta's making. However, this piece had turned out far more ethereal than either teacher or pupil had expected—as fully haunting, indeed, as the sacred Lament itself. Astonished, Ebster Oeta had petitioned to have the song performed as one of his own, to Amant's great pride. That it would bear his teacher's name did not matter to him, for he was still a boy and learning. He had been elated to have it performed at all.

Amant sighed when he began to play, remembering how the music had dogged him day and night when he was writing the piece. Although he had never told Oeta about it, he had dreamed of wild Aenan during the whole time he was inside the song making it, insistent and oddly joyful dreams of Aenan as a Tenebrian raider, a powerful, young, and fearless Aenan quite unlike the sad man of the Lament. He remembered listening to the Ebsters' tales about Aenan and how those tales had made him angry. As I have said, Kieldeans did not revere wild Aenan in those days before the Reconciliation. Still, he had been the chosen beloved of the Lake Mother and, for that reason, the Kieldeans tolerated that he should be remembered. Little Nowa, when he first arrived at the Ebsters' Hall, had become furious at the impiety and the insult the Ebsters gave to wild Aenan; yet he said nothing. He consoled himself with repeating the *Haaimikin Oide's* description of Aenan under his breath: "our warrior, our son, a father of many, ever straight and ever true in his words." Whenever the Ebsters would call the Lake Mother such things as the "kind sister of Death, who brought the spring after each winter, who helped souls who had died to enter the Sea of Sansel's Net," Amant called to mind the *Haaimikin Oide's* description of her—"wicked woman" it said, "seducer of our son, who promises life everlasting but cannot find it, who, with a dancing song on her lips, a stranger to modesty and a sister to evil, stole our son from us."

Thus did Amant grow up with both faces of each sacred guardian stamped in his heart. He knew the warrior-Aenan and the wanderer-Aenan, he knew the gentle-Trost and the dancing-Trost, and he found truth in both sides of each. It is from this dual and intimate knowledge that he wrote his greatest music, those songs that would Reconcile one half to the other. It was from this double understanding that he had written the dirge that surprised his teacher and that, to this day, bears witness to the budding power of his gift for song—his orphic's heart.

Amant stopped playing. His fingers were too stiff, and the sound of the viola was getting muddy.

Dusk had grown into dark, and the cold had become frigid. He could hear the couple returning from the grove; their murmuring voices seemed near. He stood, stretched, and put the viola away.

The driver called to his passengers. He told them they would travel through the night and should reach Kheon by sunrise. Amant clambered inside the wagon, followed by his fellow travelers. He smiled at the man and woman. But the couple did not respond. The man took a blanket from one of their boxes, and the two huddled under it.

Amant laid himself down on the floor of the carrier beside the hatch at the end. He pulled his coat about him and used his satchel as a headrest. Above, outside the canvas, the sky was rose-colored, edged in a dark blue. Slowly, the blue hardened into violet, which was swallowed by night's indigo. Amant tried to watch for the first stars and then for the constellations, but he fell asleep before even the littlest of them appeared.

☆

THE boy-who-was-thrown-away found himself in a hallway, alone. He had never seen this place before. The highly polished floors were wooden; the walls, too, were wooden. There were several closed doors, and he found himself standing in front of one of them. He pushed it open and went inside. The only thing in the room was a huge, snowy bed, blanketed in white. The bed was not empty. He saw—Osei! His heart started pounding with expectation and joy. He had found her, at last!

She was asleep, cosseted by the white blankets and white pillow mountains. Billowing sheets, spotless, seamless, and terribly white, covered her, except for her dark and rosy face and her curly, cinnamon-highlighted hair. He stood beside the bed and touched her forehead. She was feverish. She turned over at his touch, then over again, but did not wake.

He sat on the edge of the bed beside her and pressed his cheek to her hot face. He did not know why he needed to do this, but as soon as he did, he started crying for her because he knew she was ill, very ill.

Just then, she opened her eyes, startling him. Her eyes were that odd color he had dreamed of before, almost white, yet bluish, something like thick ice. Her blank gaze scared him so he tried to smile, to reassure both himself and her. But the look in her eyes was of terror. The ice of her iris grew dark with pupil and she sat up, backing deep into the pillows away from him.

He murmured that she ought not be afraid, that he had come home, that he had come home to her at last. But he spoke to her in the language of the *dovai*, as if she could understand it, as his *dovai*-sisters would have, and as if he had forgotten any other tongue. For, indeed, when he opened his mouth to speak so that she could understand, the only words that would come to him were the words of the *dovai*: "⋀⋀⋎⅂⟋ℐℙ⟨⟍⟍⅁∪⟍⅌⟍ℐ∪⅁," meaning, "Be well, my sister."

Of course, these strange sounds frightened her all the more. She flailed out at him with her small fists when he tried to feed her a mug of hot broth. Where the broth had come from he did not know,

but he insisted that she sip it. Somehow, he knew
it would help her.

She pushed the mug away, spitting the broth at
him. He jumped back, wiping it off his face, upset. She would die if she did not eat. He knew she
was dying, and it was up to him to help her, to
bring her back from the Shore of Sansel's Sea.
Death would come soon to fetch her away.

And then, suddenly, he was walking up and
down the dark beach of Death's abode with her.
He knew that the only way he could save her
would be through his *dowanaten*—yet how, how?
He paced back and forth at her side, wondering
and fearing because the *dowanaten* seemed, somehow, to have deserted him. She was ignoring his
presence too, no matter what he did, no matter
how he pleaded with her. She looked steadily out
at the low, flat surf, which rolled in over the glassy
sand flats, spreading thin and clear across the
gray earth, then washing back out again. The sand
had no shells in it; the water had no seaweed or
fish or mollusks of any kind. Barren stone, crystalline water, and a dark sky, no sounds except a
scanty, whistling wind and the "plat, plat" of their
feet padding in the wet earth . . . the roll of the
Sea, endless, distant, cold, and hopeless. What could
he do? What?

Amant woke to the ocean's voice. A few moments passed before he knew that he was indeed
awake and that he was still in the carrier on his
way to Kheon. The strange shore and the stranger
room where he had found Osei were gone. The
carrier shuddered and rolled along the rough road.
The sky had lost all but one star, and the moon's

bright eye was fading. He tried to sit up and found himself weighted down by something like a warm stone on his chest, almost as if his dream had come to sit there. The stone moved. He frowned and tried to sit again. The stone acquired a head, two black, gold-speckled eyes, and a wet nose that touched his cheek. The teka yawned, showing her fangs; then she got up off his chest to crawl down beside him and wedge herself under his arm, against his side.

Amant sat, disturbing the teka's newfound nest. He picked the tiny thing up and swiftly deposited her into his hood. As he did this, he glanced over at his traveling companions. Neither of them had moved, and he let out his breath, which he had unconsciously been holding. He pressed his hand against his breast, where his heart beat too fast. The dream and the reappearance of the teka made him feel a little afraid and disoriented. He did not want anyone to see the animal and report it to the ci'esti of Kheon; he thought he could not bear to have the teka taken from him now. As if the animal sensed his fear, she settled into the hood and did not move.

The carrier swayed. Amant steadied himself against one bench. Kneeling, he held onto the back door of the wagon and looked out, only to find himself suspended over sheer cliffs, which seemed to drop from under the carrier's wheels straight into the sea. The road wound on behind the carrier, like an ever-diminishing rope of white, twisting and turning to follow the edge of the earth and finally vanishing over a distant rise. The cliffs jutted out into the waters, their faces jagged and black, battered by the water that curled in white breakers around their feet. The steady roll of the sea's voice was far, far-off and the sea air was brisk.

The constant wind made the canvas canopy flap; it blew the boy's hair back off his face, slapped his cheeks, and made him feel as if he were back in Mossdon, on Oeta's terrace in the dawn light, watching the sun rise. Finally, hungry, he unwrapped what little was left of the seed-cake and ate it, as the wagon swung around a curve and began to descend the hill.

Halfway down the steep incline, the carrier passed a field that was fenced in by a low rock wall. The grass grew high, but not high enough to hide the scattered stones there. The stones were all the same, except for their sizes; black and shiny, they ranged from as tall as a full-grown man to as small as a rabbit. For a moment, he thought that they were wishing stones, until he saw that they were uncarved. No chiseled bears, or lambs, or bullocks, or frogs, no carven owls (the traditional emblems of the Lake Mother of Wyessa) decorated their faces. They were smooth, featureless, black, and silent. Not wishing stones, but grave-stones.

A little beyond the graveyard, over the curve of grass, he saw the roofs of Kheon Kield. As the carrier then descended toward the cape, listing at an angle, Amant could see the whole of the Kield spread out before him.

The roofs were tiled in yellow. Every single roof, every single tile, was glazed in a yellow that was more vibrant than any the boy had ever seen.

He thought it looked as if the people had stolen a swatch of the sun for their homes. In full daylight, the Kield was difficult to gaze upon for very long, so dazzling and bright was this color.

Amant squinted, shading his eyes with one hand. Oddly, the sight of Kheon made him ill. The seed-cake sat on his stomach like a stone, as heavy as when the teka had rested on his chest that morn. Kheon was so large! He had never in his life seen such a confusion of roofs, such a weltering jumble of buildings and villas. And there were so many ships in the harbor, it seemed a forest of jibs and sails! The winding, narrow streets looked jammed with people. He had never imagined it so large. At that time, when the boy-who-was-thrown-away was young, Kheon was as large as seven or eight Bildrons, or three Mossdon Kields stacked one next to the other. To this day, Kheon sprawls from one side of the cape to the other and even out to the very brink of the land where it meets the sea.

The carrier dipped and straightened itself, trundling down the hill toward the immense and awful Kield. Amant's courage sank; he wondered why he had ever left Bildron—or Mossdon, for that matter. How would it be at the Academe? If they did not take him in, how would he fill his plate and keep himself clothed? Where would he find a warm bed? He thought of the Drake, but his experience with the ci'esti in Bildron and the fact that he harbored the little teka made him wary. Grimly, he watched the carrier take him to Kheon.

The teka crawled up his back, her claws prickling through all the layers of his clothing. The nick of tiny nails itched. He twisted around. The animal peeked out of the folds of the hood and licked his neck under his ear; then she nestled down into the cowl's darkness.

"What've ye got there?" said the woman to the boy. She and her companion had waked. The man was up, rummaging in their boxes. The woman stared at Amant from the tumbled blanket where she sat.

The man turned around. He tugged at the woman's sleeve and shook his head. The wagon rocked. He steadied himself, straightened his brown jacket, slicked back his hair, and helped his companion to a seat on the bench. She dropped her gaze and said nothing more. The man rolled their blanket up and tied it with twine. He sat next to the woman and held her hand.

"It's a puppy," said Amant.

But neither the man nor the woman responded to him. He wondered at their silence. It relieved him that they did not question him further, but it also made him feel hurt. He was still puzzling over this, when the carrier passed through the open gates of the Kield. Once inside, they pulled off the cobbled street into a yard where other wagons were parked. The driver unhooked the back of the carrier and helped his passengers alight. Amant paid the fee and swung his satchel onto his shoulder with care, mindful of the creature in his hood.

The carrier had come to the porter's inn of Kheon, named Brother's Home. It was a long villa with many windows, all on one floor. A few moments after the carrier stopped and the passengers had gotten out, a lively man, who put Amant in mind of the Pocket's proprietor, appeared and handed the three passengers each a tankard of ale from a tray. He told them that he was the porter of Kheon and that he would be pleased to offer them a meal and a bed for the night.

Amant thanked the man and told him that he had a letter of introduction to the Academe and hoped to find food and lodging there—could he ask what way was best to walk to the Academe?

The woman traveler gasped, loud enough for Amant to hear. He turned. She stared at him, this time with unmistakable fright. Her companion put his arm around her waist and walked her toward the porter's inn. He gave Amant a hard and defensive glare. The woman trembled, spilling her ale.

As soon as the couple had gone, the porter laughed. "Must be folk from Cuto," he said. He shook his head.

"Why?" asked the boy.

"They weren't too friendly on the trip, I expect?"

"No. But why? What did I do?"

"Nothing, I daresay. They thought, no doubt, that you were a ci'esti—from the way you are dressed, understand. Your bearing. But now, they know you for a chanter! To some people, mostly those in the south reaches, like Cuto Kield, a chanter is dangerous. Chanters know the secrets of the earth and can steal a soul from out the warm body before one would even suspect. Have you never heard this?"

Amant shook his head.

The porter unpocketed a pipe and tapped it clean. He shrugged. "Well, that is what some folk believe. Nonsense, of course, but those two are young and haven't seen much of Gueame save Cuto, I daresay." He leaned forward and whispered, "Their heads are stuffed full of dangers!" He laughed. "So . . . you've come to Kheon for the Academe?"

"Yes."

"And where do you hail from?"

"The Ebsters' Hall, in Mossdon."

"So far? Quite some distance, for nothing."

"Pardon?" said Amant.

"You've traveled a long way, for nothing. The Academe is no longer a school; there has been illness there or something. Weeds grow high where once there was a garden." He reached into his pocket and pulled out a small sack of shag. As he filled the pipe's bowl, he nodded to himself. "No music there, anymore. No more teachers," he said. "Haven't the Ebsters heard?"

Before Amant could answer, the driver of the carrier walked up and put his empty tankard back on the tray at the porter's feet. He put his hand on the man's shoulder and said something to him in a whisper. The porter lit his pipe and listened, nodded, glanced at the boy. The driver left, to lead the mules into the stable.

The porter smiled at the boy-who-was-thrown-away and blew out a puff of scented smoke. "My brother tells me that Seftenir would have us be hosts to you for as long as you wish."

"I . . ." said Amant, confused. He felt the blood rise to his face. "I don't know. . . ."

The man frowned. "Seftenir, the porter of Bildron. She is our sister. . . ."

"Sister!" Amant stepped back. Now he was truly confused. None of his memories included uncles.

The man cocked his head. "Not by blood, certainly. We three take care of one another, my brother, Seftenir, and I. So! Have a meal with us. Stay until you can decide what you want to do. Perhaps you should go back to Mossdon? Or maybe you would stay in Kheon, eh? I heard the Drake seeks a new chanter to teach at the Academe. Or maybe you would rather take billet on a ship and visit the Alentines, or go to the end of the world?" The porter laughed. "Come, come, whatever you choose, spend a little time with my brother and me. You're a young man and all your life ahead. No need for rushing."

Amant nodded slowly and followed the porter and his silent brother to the inn. As he ate with them, he listened to the porter speak about Kheon. Like its sister Kields of Mossdon and Adeo, Kheon was a busy port. Built into the crook of West Rock Cape, it sits upon cliffs above the White Sea and commands a far view, overlooking narrow, rugged beaches. Being a western Kield, it is warmer all year than its northern sister, Mossdon, but not as warm as the fair Alentines. The villas and buildings of Kheon have several stories to them and are built of a local clay, which fires to a yellow brick. So, not only are the roof tiles brilliant, but also the walls and façades, except where there are paintings of seashells done or mosaics of sea creatures inlaid. The people of Kheon are fond of such things.

Amant listened and ate and was thus well-cared for during his first few hours in Kheon. The two

brothers, whose names have been forgotten over
time, filled his stomach with the bounty of their
larder and his mind with the bounty of their fancy.
By mid-afternoon the boy felt as if Kheon might
not be so awful a place after all and, bidding the
brothers a thank-you and goodbye, he set off on
the road they had shown him, to find the Academe. No matter what the rumors, no matter what
the porter said, Amant could not leave Kheon
without seeing the school and trying to find out
what had happened to the orphics who had once
been so revered.

He shook hands with the brothers and bowed to
each as he left their doorstep. With his satchel in
hand and the teka asleep in his cowl, he crossed
the front yard of the inn and strode out onto the
now-crowded street. As he turned a corner, a familiar voice caught his ear and he glanced quickly
over his shoulder, puzzled by familiarity in so
unfamiliar a place. Then he flattened himself
against a wall in surprise, for just pulling into the
innyard was a small wagon full of the jongleurs
who had begged him to sing with them in Bildron.
He caught his breath, but then relaxed. They had
not seen him. Waiting a moment until the street
was fairly busy and the jongleurs out of sight, he
hurried on his way. Something about those jongleurs made him uneasy, even though he remembered their saying they were native to Kheon.
He did not want them to find him, nor did he
want them to ask him about the night he had
deserted their round. He thought they would ask
about the *dowanaten* of that night, and he did not
know how he could explain it to them.

Walking swiftly, he followed the street the porter had pointed out, no matter where it strayed—followed it as it took him past busy shops that sold fine cloth, down along the harbor where sailors gossiped and eyed him as if they had it in mind to test his mettle, through the open market square loud with the sing-song of merchants hawking wares, across quiet sections where people sat on doorstoops and talked and drank something hot from a common pot. Every now and then, he would glance behind him, but his uneasiness seemed misplaced. The jongleurs were not to be seen.

He walked for what seemed O, so long a time—long enough for the sun to begin setting toward night—before he came to the narrow gate that led into the yard and thence to the door of the Academe.

6

Osei

THE GATE OF the Academe was not locked.
Amant stood beside it for a few moments,
staring into the overgrown yard and at the tall
door at the end of the walk. People pushed and
jostled down the busy street, paying the boy no
mind. Anxiously, he glanced behind him, but none
of the faces he saw were familiar. He breathed
deeply and wiped his brow with his sleeve.

Finally, he pulled the gate latch up and went
inside. The walk to the door was made of slate;
true to what the porter of Kheon had said, the
garden was wild and unattended. Straggling vines
of the istic berry plant crawled up one side of the
stone building. A few brown leaves clung to the
vine's finger-roots, which had dug into both rock
and mortar. Twined in among the berry vine was
a web of night-tongues, but none of the white
flowers were blooming. Though he was but several feet from the busy street beyond the Academe's gate, it was quiet in the garden. The silence
made him move more slowly than he had been
moving. He felt a stillness inside himself that he

welcomed after the hectic mood of the streets and his worry over the jongleurs.

He went up to the door and stopped. He stared at the knocker, afraid to touch it. It was carved of an ebon wood and shaped in the head of a bullock. A ring of silver in the bullock's nose served as the knocker, and silver had been used to form two tapering horns. He had seen precious silver objects in Mossdon, but they all had been sacred objects, consecrated to the souls of the dead, or else dedicated to the Lake Mother. Never had he seen silver used for such a common thing as a door knocker.

He did not want to touch it but, at last, he did. He stepped back from the door as it swung inward. A lanky man appeared. He was tall and bald; a suggestion of hair, like dark eyelashes, edged his scalp about the ears. His skin was dark, almost too dark in places, as if he were bruised. His eyes had a quickness to their glance, a sharp, bright, and appraising look. The timbre of his voice was low and deep when he said, "It is supper time—what do you want?"

Amant was so nervous that he did not know how to answer such a gruff and unexpected greeting. So, he did not say anything.

Neither did the man.

The two stood facing one another, in silence, until the man began to shut the door.

Then, Amant said, "Please . . . please. I've come from Mossdon."

"And? So?"

"With a letter. From Ebster Oeta."

"Oeta?" The man frowned. "Oeta? Well, well . . .

what could he want from me, after so many years? Eh? Show the letter."

Amant put his satchel on the ground and took out his viola case, where he had put the letter. He handed the sealed parchment to the man, who broke it open, read it, folded it without speaking, and glared at the boy.

Under such hostile scrutiny, Amant wondered what he had done wrong. As he stood there, looking down at his boots and wishing himself far away, the teka chose to squirm and resettle herself in his hood. He winced as the prickling claws nicked his back.

The movement did not go unnoticed. The man said, "What is it?"

"My feet hurt," said Amant quickly. He stepped backward, hoping the stranger could not see the lump in the hood. "I'm tired and I'm chilly and my feet hurt."

The man frowned again and pushed the door open. "Come in, then," he said.

Thus, Amant Wuulf-Moas entered the Academe of West Rock Cape. The hall at the entrance looked onto a large, whitewashed room that held a few floor cushions. The man led the boy across the empty room and down another hall, which had wide windows. The windows looked out on a yard that was paved with mosaic stones. The mosaic figured someone—a face, or two faces perhaps, or perhaps a creature; Amant could not make it out. In the center of the mosaic yard, he spied the Academe's wishing stone. It was a small one, compared to the one he had seen in the Ebsters' Hall, rounded but thin, like a dark, flattened, tattooed finger pointing at the sky.

The lanky man stopped walking and showed Amant a bench beside a closed door. "Sit here," he said. "I will be back for you in a moment." And the man went through the door, leaving the boy to himself.

Amant set his satchel on the bench and went over to the window; he wanted to see what the mosaic pictured.

The yard was not empty. Beside the high wall that separatd the yard from the villa next door, stood a child. The child was alone. Dressed in winter clothing—thick trousers, a quilted jacket, and a fur cap with ear pieces—the child had a large ball in hand and was bouncing it against the wall. Whether the child was a girl or boy, Amant could not tell. Soon, the child stopped playing and sat down on top of the ball. What little of the child's face could be seen over the scarf was splotched red from the cold.

Amant knocked on the window and waved. He decided that the child was a girl, because something about her reminded him of Osei. Or maybe it was that this child reminded him of the sisters he had once had when he lived in the *dovai*—six of them, his *dovai*-parents' girls, some younger than he, most older. The child in the mosaic yard stood up, letting the ball roll away. She ran to the window and beckoned him outside, pointing across the yard to where there was a door. He shook his head. She pointed again. He shook his head no.

The girl shrugged and turned her back on him.

She scuffled over to her ball and began bouncing it, ignoring him.

Amant glanced at the door where the man had gone. It was still closed. He could hear nothing beyond it, not even a murmur. After some time had passed, time enough for afternoon to turn to evening, he decided he was tired of waiting, tired of always sitting and waiting outside some door, waiting for someone to come for him, whether it was an Ebster or the Drake of Bildron or this man who had, perhaps, been a friend to Oeta long ago. Besides, it was getting dark. Amant walked around the hallway to the door and went into the yard.

When the girl saw him, she threw her ball to him over the wishing stone. He caught it. She laughed, sending breath-smoke through the wool scarf. He threw the ball back and she caught it, and so they played several minutes back and forth until, wihout warning, the teka leaped out from the boy's hood. She landed clumsily atop the wishing stone.

The girl screeched as the teka launched herself from her slippery purchase on the stone, flying up to the wall and then, vanishing in the dusk. The wool scarf slipped from the child's face.

Amant stood still; the shock of seeing her face kept him rooted to the pavement, while the teka was lost to sight. The girl stared back at him. She was Osei.

She ran to the door and once inside, slammed it behind her. For a moment, the boy did not move. Then he ran after her, calling her name. He had not meant to scare her by his call, but she ran even faster when she heard him. He followed her to a staircase and then up it, listening for her footsteps. He heard nothing and marveled at her silence. When he reached the second-story landing, she had disappeared. He heard no sound and saw no sign of her at all.

He stood in the hall, undecided and confused. Surely, he had seen Osei—he could not mistake her! But, he wondered, how could she be so little, still? He reckoned the time and found that she would have to be nearly a young woman by now, as he was soon to be a man. Yet, he had seen a child, and it was she, he was sure of it. Could he be dreaming? He shook his head. He was not asleep. Besides, he told himself, how could a dream throw a ball? The ball had felt real in his hands. He peered down the second story. Where had she gone? There were three doors to his left; the door closest to him was closed, the other two were open.

Should he try to find her? Or should he return to the bench where the man had left him and wait, then ask the man who the child had been? He stood and wondered. Meantime, the sun had set completely and the hall was dark. He was about to leave when someone's singing came softly from the open door at the far end of the hall. The voice was a soprano, and he smiled to himself. The girl—Osei?—was teasing him. He moved toward the sound, stepping lightly across the polished wooden floor. He glanced into the first open door and saw a small, bare room, bare save for a strange instrument and a set of cushions in neat rows before it. Fascinated, he stopped. The instrument was strange to him: a wooden frame in the shape of bullock's horns stood supporting a crossbeam.

From the beam, a set of bells was suspended. They ranged in size from a tiny thing, no bigger than Amant's thumb, to a long one, half the length of his arm. Transparent, they seemed made of blown glass, etched with a fine, silver tracery depicting flowers and treble half-moons. Clapperless, they were fragile-seeming, but when Amant touched one, they felt as hard as diamond.

He wanted to tap the bells and hear their tones, but the singing had grown stronger; it drew him away. He went to the second open door and peeked in. The place looked to him very like Oeta's study in Mossdon, save this room was not as bare as his had been. The floor here was carpeted with two identical, thickly piled rugs of the sort for which the weavers of Adeo were known; shelves held row upon row of books; there were boxes full of seashells and baskets stuffed with odd blocks of wood. On a table in a corner there stood some small, wooden carvings: a lamb, an ebon owl, a pipe in the shape of a bear.

In another corner, shadowed by the dusk, a young woman sat on a flat, white cushion. She was singing. But this was not the child whom he had taken for Osei, but rather another, older girl. She was wrapped in a blanket and rocked herself gently back and forth. He would have left her and gone away, because she was not the child he sought, had it not been for the song she sang. The melody was the same as that of *Wild Aenan's Lament*, the very same, but it was not the Lament—the words were different and told of the Lake Mother's search for her lost child, rather than the Mother's loss of her beloved. It was a lyric Amant had never heard

before, and, as he listened, he found himself drawn
into the music until he too was singing.

And he sang, but he sang the words that he
knew; he gave her *Wild Aenan's Lament*, while she
gave him the Lake Mother's cry. The two min-
gled, harmonious; different and yet conjoined by
the melody. The young woman's voice wove high
where Amant's went low; he murmured and she
trilled; his dark, hers light; complements, as the
songs complemented one another.

The girl did not turn, nor did she show in any
way that she had noticed him. She kept on with
her own song. At times her voice grew a shade
stronger, so that his would not take over or drown
her out. When the last verse had been sung thrice,
she sighed.

Amant tried to catch his breath. The music had
constricted his heart. His mouth was dry. The
room felt warm, as if the singing had changed the
quality of the air, even the taste of it. Everything
looked sharper to him and, at the same time, less
sharp. He could not understand it, the colors of
the patterned rug flamed, but the designs had
become indistinct; the walls had turned painfully
white, so white he could no longer see the books
on the bookshelves for the glare.

The girl turned to face him. He had trouble
knowing her at first. But then, the curly dark-gilt
hair, the strangely pale eyes, the pale brown skin,
and the bow lips told him she was Osei, an older
Osei than he remembered, yet familiar, so familiar that when she got up from the cushion and
took his hands in her own, he knew he could not
be mistaken.

And somehow, as if he had been in a dream, it did not seem strange to him to meet her in this place. Nor did he marvel that she was not the child he had been seeking. She chafed his cold hands between hers and said to him, "I have waited and waited for you. How long! And now you've come."

"I've dreamed of you," he said. "Osei?"

"Yes."

"Am I dreaming again? Or is it the . . . is it a dream?"

"No."

"Osei." He slipped his arms around her and hugged her, leaning down to put his cheek against her neck for a moment. He said, "You are cold! So cold."

"I've been ill," she said.

He remembered his dream of her illness and how she would not accept his help. He stepped back to look at her, then put his hand on her brow.

Except for her coldness, she did not seem unwell. He hugged her again. She smelled of herself, a sweet and tangy fragrance that he could not describe, but which was utterly familiar to him. The odor brought him a swift memory of an afternoon when the two of them had gotten a chill that kept them tucked in bed. They had had each other for company and their toys to play with, and so they had not been lonely or sad—until the sun had gone down and the room had grown cold. Then, Osei had crept from her bed to his, dragging her blanket after her. They had snuggled under the bedclothes, she at the foot of the bed and he at the headboard. Facing each other, they had made hills and valleys with the blankets—tall mountains and lowly plains, pits and peaks. On the plains, there lived a herd of horses; these belonged to Osei. In the mountains, there lived the tekas; these belonged to Amant. They had gone about making their world and whispering to one another, planting fields and inventing Kields, creating animals and birthing people, until they had both fallen asleep.

Asleep . . . Amant decided that he must have fallen asleep, somehow. He was either sleeping or else he was caught again in the *dowanaten*, because he was not inside the Academe anymore. He was on a beach. He was on a long and empty spit of land near some great sea, and Osei was with him, at his side. They went walking barefoot on the dream-beach. He saw that they left small, uneven footprints in the sand behind them; indeed, he saw that they were leaving children's footprints. He was a child again. Osei was a child. And her eyes were not silver, but brown.

Yet, as they walked, the children grew up. Amant could feel himself getting taller. There would be a quiver inside him a shivery, quivery shake, and then a sliding up! And then—larger footprints. He glanced at Osei, meaning to say something, but his mouth would not move when he saw that she too was growing in the same rapid way. She would shiver, as if chilled, and seem to straighten her back, stiffen her spine; then, she would be—older. With each swinging step, she was less a child and more a young woman.

Suddenly, she stopped walking, and so he did

too. Her face was shaded by the low angle of the light, and although he wished to see her expression, he could only discern the line of her sharp nose and the outline of her lips and chin. Her eyes were hidden, and he could not tell if she were smiling or frowning. He reached out and turned her face toward him. The bronze light tinted her brown skin a more golden hue, golden and flat like brass. When at last she looked up, he saw that her eyes were a pale, pale color, paler than amber, paler than honey, crystalline. She appeared almost as a statue might, still and utterly calm, with skin of metal and eyes of diamond.

"Osei?" said a stranger, a new voice in the dark, seaswept land. It was a woman's voice, husky but gentle. He wanted to search out the owner of this new voice, but he could not stop staring into the strange, clear eyes of his sister-cousin who had become, all at once, so alien.

"Osei?" said the woman again. "Let him go, child. Let him return. You cannot keep him there with you."

Amant heard these words, but then the voice grew louder and so distorted that it melted into the sound of the sea that lapped at his feet. The water dabbled its foam fingers around his toes and tickled his ankles. He reached for his cousin, but she stepped away. He stumbled after her as she backed into the surf. The strong wind buffeted her, and she was lashed by the dancing foam. She waded out to her waist, rocking with the motion of the waves. He strove to follow because he thought she would be dragged under. He feared she would drown. The wind blew gouts of water high into the air. Huge sprays reached for the sky and there dissolved into mist. He felt the undertow capture him and drag him down. He fought. Sputtering, he screamed to Osei. She was floating before him, almost within reach; then she vanished.

A wave surged; he went under. He twisted and pushed back toward the surface, looking for his cousin, but in vain. The water was so cold his limbs were numb. At that moment, he felt a hand close gently around his own and give a little tug. He looked up; the surface seemed impossible to gain. He ceased fighting and drifted, expecting to drown, for the hand led him downward and not toward the sky.

"Amant?"

The boy surfaced—or at least it seemed that he did. He did not hear the terrible pounding of the sea anymore, nor did he feel the claw of the undertow dragging him down. Slowly, he became aware that he was not on any shore or beach at all. He was lying on a cushion—that same cushion upon which Osei had sat when he had sung the Lament with her in the room of the flamming-hued rugs. He sat up. He felt as if he had been asleep a long time and his forehead ached as if he had been struck. He rubbed his temples and looked around.

It was light in the room and Osei had gone. But he was not alone. A woman stood beside the cushion. She gazed out the window, until he made a slight noise, which would tell her that he had waked.

She glanced at him. She was not very tall, but

there was a grace in her that my great-great-grandfather claimed made her appear tall. Her jet hair was long and ungathered, falling straight to her waist. He had seldom seen anyone wear their long hair loose and free, without braids, as she did. He thought it odd, but pretty. He noticed too that this tall woman, who was not truly tall, had the same oddly pale eyes that he had seen in Osei's face in his dream. This stranger's irises were as clear as glass, stained with the faintest trace of a watery blue, and rimmed round with a line of indigo. Her gaze seemed to shoot directly through him, and he felt as if he had become as transparent as the woman's eyes. This feeling frightened him so much that he lay back down and averted his face.

Am I dreaming still? he thought. *Shall I be trapped forever in the dowanaten? Is this what happens to those granted wild Aenan's power who never learn its proper use? Truly, then, is the Kieldean's insight a curse.*

Meanwhile, the woman knelt beside the cushion on one knee and put her hand flat on his forehead. She asked, "Are you better now?"

When he did not reply, she took her hand away and sat on the floor with her legs crossed. She said, "Did the Ebsters never teach you manners?"

Startled he glanced at her again. Her voice was husky but gentle—the same voice he had heard in the *dowanaten* dream. He sat up again and said, "Where is Osei?" He did not expect an answer that made sense, really. He thought he might still be asleep. But the room and the woman and the cushion beneath him seemed real. So he thought there could be no harm in asking after his sister-cousin.

To the boy's surprise, the woman said, "She is in her room. You may see her, later."

"She is here? Truly?"

"You saw her."

"Y . . . yes. . . ." said Amant, unsure. "Did you . . . did you. . . ." He was not able to frame a question that would answer his uncertainty.

The woman said, "Osei is not well."

"That's what she said." Amant closed his eyes. He told himself that he had fallen asleep and that this woman had found him, asleep on the cushion. There had been no beach. There had been no drowning, no salt spray, no sand. When he heard the stranger's voice, it was merely because she had been trying to wake him—or perhaps talking to Osei. Shakily, he stood. He would have to beg the Lake Mother to take away the insight soon, before it took over his whole life. Trying to appear calm, he said, "What is wrong with Osei?"

The woman did not answer him. Instead, she asked, "Did you bring the teka with you?"

He stared at the woman, frozen by her question. Had the creature been seen in Kheon? Had this stranger found it? Had she told the ci'esti? Would the teka be drowned? "What?" he said.

"There is a teka in the courtyard," said the woman patiently. "She is waiting for something. Or someone. Is she waiting for you?"

Amant hurried over to the window. To his surprise, rain fell, and it was no longer evening but dawn—a dark and stormy dawn. The mosaic stones were slick with a sheet of water. Yet, despite the dark and the rain, Amant could make out several things—one, the teka, prowling about pacing. Two, from the boy's second-story vantage, he could now understand what it was the tesserae of the mosaic figured. It was a picture of wild Aenan. Seated in a forest of jade-flowering trees, his mouth open in song, Aenan had his hands stretched out to several carnelian birds, which hopped at his feet or flew about his head. At his elbow, the artist had placed an obsidian-stone teka. In a corner of the yard, a white-quartz child stood, shyly hidden behind some bamboo trees. In another corner, a woman wearing bluestone covered her face with her sandstone hands. In fact, the whole yard's floor was a large illustration depicting the story of how wild Aenan went searching for his lost child. The Tales of Kheon said he asked the birds, in song, whither his young one's soul had gone.

Amant smiled and leaned out the window to see the mosaic better. Of course the Academe would have such a depiction, he thought, for orphics who were not Ebsters sometimes claimed a kinship with the first orphic of Gueame—Aenan. Seeing the face of Aenan gave the boy a sudden moment of peace, as if he had discovered a treasure amid uncertainty.

The teka stopped prowling. She leaped back on top of the wishing stone and stared up at him. She mewled. The sound echoed loudly in the court-yard, bouncing off the walls of the Academe.

He glanced at the woman with the straight, dark hair. She had folded up the blanket under which he had slept and was placing it back in a cupboard on the wall. He tiptoed to the door and ran down to the courtyard.

Now, who was this woman with the eyes of ice and the ungathered jet hair? If you know the Tales of Kheon well, perhaps you have already guessed. Or if you are a southerner, perhaps you are one of her kin. Or if you are a northerner, as I am, born and bred to the snows of Marridon, the withering winds of Pacot, or the rainy autumns in Bildron where the winters are long and grim, perhaps you have heard of her deeds. But if you are none of these, then you will have to follow along with my telling and see her as she was in those days when no one knew her name.

7

*The Mistress
of the Academe*

THE WIND WAS beating clouds quickly across the sky. It was a moaning wind, and it stung Amant's eyes as he stood in the mosaic courtyard with his hands in his pockets and his collar pulled up around his face. The teka had returned from hunting with a half-eaten quarry—the head and spine of a field mouse. The hunter sat on top of the wishing stone, watching Amant. The boy-who-was-thrown-away took a step toward the stone. The teka stopped eating and glared at him with its gold-black eyes. It growled in a low and gravelly voice, warning him off. He stood still and waited. The teka went back to her meal. The boy took another step. The animal growled and glared. The boy stopped. The teka went back to its meal.

He did not know how long they played this game, while he stood in the wet, getting wetter, but it was long enough for him to become soaked. Then, for a moment, all the sky brightened; a clap and crash followed with a sweep of heavier rain that gusted across the mosaic floor. The game ended. The teka whined and cringed. She leaped at the boy and attached herself to his coat sleeve. Another clap of thunder sent the animal scrambling into the cave of his hood, which Amant had neglected to pull up when he had run into the rainy yard. He walked to the wishing stone and nudged the remains of the mouse off, letting the corpse drop onto the pavement.

He knelt before the carved, black stone, his heart pounding erratically. He had only been allowed to make a wish upon a wishing stone once before, in the Ebsters' Hall. Sprouting from the center of the Ebsters' court, tall, thin, and black, the stone had seemed somehow awful with its elaborate carvings of the bullock, the lamb, the frog, and the owl—symbols of the Lake Mother's power. Awful because servants were allowed to approach it only once in all their lives; awful because Oeta had taught the boy—as we are taught to this day—that the Lake Mother was bound by ancient promise to fulfill a person's wish, particularly if that wish was made with sincerity and a full heart. Yet, her ways of answering are often strange. If you are not careful with your wish, you might be unpleasantly surprised by her answer. Amant knelt and thought about what his wish should be. He had assumed he would ask the Lake Mother to take away the *dowanaten*. But . . .

Amant shifted his position; his knees were sore, and he was soaked. Inside his hood, the teka mewled, low and pitifully. The boy placed his hands over the owl's eyes in the stone, bowed his head, and wished that he might be able to help Osei. In the moment when he bowed his head, this wish seemed stronger than anything.

He stood up, stamping blood back into his
numbed feet. The woman with the strange eyes
stood in the door of the courtyard, clutching her
robe closed, its long folds gathered against her
legs by the wind's force. She beckoned to him, and
he ran across the wet pavement. For a moment,
the sky brightened again with lightning, which
was followed instantly by a thunderclap so loud its
boom seemed to be inside the boy's head rather
than in the sky. He yanked the door shut behind
him, damping the wind's howl and the thunder's
fury. The woman locked the door.

She turned to him and said, "You are Ebster
Oeta's nephew? So his letter told us."

Amant blushed, since this was not the truth.
But, in accordance with his teacher's wishes, he
nodded. He stared at the wall, avoiding the woman's gaze.

She said, "Osei has told me you are her brother."

"Cousin," he said. "We are cousins. Where is
she? What is wrong with her? Let me see her. . . ."

The teka poked her flat head out from the
hood and shook off rain drops, then crawled onto
the boy's shoulder. He pulled her away from his
shoulder and put her on the floor by his feet. He
wondered what the woman would say about the
creature, but instead was surprised to hear the
woman ask, "How are you Osei's cousin? Giolla's
nephew died."

"No," said Amant. "She thought I had died.
Where is Aunt Giolla? Is she here, too?"

"She told us her nephew had been killed in the
raid on Bildron. But Osei said no. She always

insisted, and I believed her, because she ought to know."

The woman folded her arms and watched the teka gnaw at the boy's toes. When the animal began to chew on the sole of one boot, Amant bent over and picked her up. He said to the woman, "Who are you? What is your name?"

She answered, "Here, I am the Mistress of the Academe."

"What will you do?" he demanded.

"Do?" She smiled. She took off her robe and folded it over one arm. It was made of a heavy material, as were her trousers and tunic; the clothes looked very warm, especially because they were all black. She said, "I was going to get some breakfast. Are you hungry?"

"Yes," he said. "But . . ."

"Well, come along. Your teka is hungry, too. They always are when they are pups."

"How . . . how do you know?"

"I raised one, once," she said.

"But I thought . . . I thought you might take her away . . . to the Drake . . . or ci'esti. . . ."

"Why would I do that?"

"Because . . . the Tales . . . I mean, I thought the Drake might drown . . . I was told there weren't any left, as the Tale says. . . ." Amant trailed off.

The woman nodded. "There are not many tekas in some Kields. In some, there are no more. . . ." She glanced at the animal in Amant's arms. "Wild beautiful creatures and too loyal for their own good. . . ." The Mistress walked down the hall toward the bench where Amant had been told to wait. His belongings were still sitting beside the door.

He retrieved his satchel and asked, "What do you mean?"

The woman opened the door and motioned Amant inside. She slipped her robe back on as she followed after him. "They will die for you. I have seen it happen." She shut the door. They were standing in a narrow room that had a long table in it, near to filling it. The table was surrounded by benches. The painted walls of the room bore murals showing a group of chanters. One played a flute; two, viols; and one a drum. The boy did not have time to examine the revel closely before the woman led him through another doorway and into a kitchen.

The man who had first greeted Amant was there, sitting at the hearth, his shoulders wrapped in a shawl. He was nursing a cup of tea, staring at the fire.

Amant sat down where the Mistress told him to—at the small table in the corner of the kitchen. The man looked up and said to the boy, "Where did you go last night? I told you to wait for me." He half-turned toward the woman. "Where did you find him?"

"Upstairs," she said.

"Upstairs?" The man glared at Amant, frowning. "Why did you not wait, as I told you?"

"Emrack," said the Mistress. "I think she called him."

The man took a breath, then let it out. "What do you mean by that, Amarra?"

"What I say." The Mistress turned to Amant.

"Did Osei speak with you? Did she call you upstairs?"

Uncomfortable, Amant shifted in his chair and cast his gaze down to the floor. He was still not sure what he had seen or whether Osei had been a dream or not. The Mistress said that Osei was there, in the Academe . . . but, what about the beach? Where was that? How had he gotten there? How had he gotten back? He opened his mouth to try to answer the woman, when the man named Emrack said, "Are you not Nowa, from Mossdon?"

"Yes . . . I have been called Nowa. . . ."

"Are you not Oeta's nephew?"

Amant blushed. "Yes . . . no . . . I mean . . ."

"How do you know of Osei?"

Amant frowned at the man's brusque manner. The boys squared his shoulders and said, "She is my cousin. Where is she?"

Emrack shook his head. "Cousin? Her only cousin died in the raid of Bildron, seasons ago."

"I did not die," said Amant.

Emrack frowned. "Giolla said . . ."

"Aunt was mistaken," said the boy. "Where is she? Let me talk to her—or Osei—they will know me."

Emrack stood up. "Giolla is dead." He turned his back on the boy and moved closer to the hearth. He stretched his knobby fingers out to the warmth and flexed them.

Amant folded his arms. He sat with his head bowed a few minutes. The teka padded across the table, onto his shoulder, and then crawled into his hood. He said, "I'm sorry."

Emrack gave a small shrug and rubbed his elbows. He kept his gaze on the fire.

The Mistress of the Academe walked up behind the man and put her arm around his waist. After a few minutes, she gently urged him back into his chair. As she handed him another teacup, she asked Amant again, "What did our cousin say to you?"

He sighed. "In the courtyard, when I first saw her, she . . ."

Emrack seemed to grow instantly older as Amant spoke. His long, dark visage became darker and longer. He said, "You could not have seen her in the yard. Not in the yard! She is too ill."

"But . . . there was someone . . . a little girl. I thought . . ."

"No!" said the man.

"I saw her," said Amant, stubbornly. His face felt hot. "I am not a liar."

"No?" said Emrack, turning suddenly. His voice was thin and screechy with emotion. "You claim to be my child's cousin, yet you also claim to be Oeta's nephew. Which is it, boy? Or don't you know one lie from another?"

"That's enough," said the Mistress. "Leave the young man alone, Emrack. I'm sure there is an explanation." She touched Amant's shoulder and pointed to a stack of bowls on a counter top. "Have some food. Then, afterward, we will talk."

"Explanation? I will not be quiet, Amarra," said Emrack, angrily. "The boy lies. When I tell him to wait, he goes wandering off to bother my poor child." He pointed at Amant. "Who are you? Young Wuulf-Moas died. And Oeta . . . he was my good friend, years ago. I know he had no brothers or sisters. There could be no nephew for him."

Amant clenched his hands and stood up. "As you will," he said stiffly. He picked up his satchel. "I am not Amant then—nor the Ebster Oeta's nephew, I am

\\?Φ(~ʃ\\(Φ~()∠(५|)υ(υ((ʃυ/γ??--

The teka began to hiss and then to howl in a low, uncanny voice from her hiding place in the boy's cowl.

The Mistress of the Academe put down the bowls she was carrying and stepped between the man and the angry boy. She glared at them both in turn, as if they were little children, and said, "If you must argue, take it outside to the rain and let the storm have your ill will. I don't want it in here!"

Abashed, Amant sat down.

Emrack shook his head slowly and sighed. He reached for the woman's small hand and held it in both of his own, hiding her slender fingers in his knobby ones. He said, "I'm sorry, sorry. But, Amarra, the boy . . ."

"I'm not a liar," said Amant.

The Mistress hushed him with one glance of her pale, pale eyes. She squeezed the man's hand and let him go. "I think we might listen to the young man's explanation before we send him away, don't you, Emrack?"

The man nodded, curtly.

"I didn't lie," said Amant. "Oeta thought it would help me, here at the Academe, if he said that I was his nephew. He has been more than good to me, and treated me as an uncle might. He taught me all he could at Mossdon. But I am not, truly, his nephew."

Emrack looked the boy over. "Help you? Why would he think such a story, such a letter, would help you?"

"Help me to enter the Academe. . . ."

Emrack laughed shortly and shook his head again. "There is no Academe. Surely they must have heard this in Mossdon? I thought the Ebsters would have known by now that there is no more music, no more life, here." He touched Amarra's cheek and patted her shoulder. "I must rest."

She nodded. "I'll be with you, in a bit."

He smiled and left the kitchen, walking slowly and with a slight shuffle.

Amant stared after the man. He stood up, as if to follow. The teka hissed from the pocket of his hood.

"Sit down," said the Mistress, irritably. "You've upset Emrack enough as it is. Sit down and eat. Here." She handed him something wet and slippery—a raw liver, deep brick red and still bloody. Astonished, Amant stared at her.

She laughed. "For your angry friend in the hood. *Your* breakfast is on the table." She pointed to a steaming bowl. He peeked into it cautiously: fish stew; pieces of squid and whole shrimp floated in a rich broth with varied vegetables. He put the liver down on the hearthstones. The teka scrambled over his shoulder, nicking him in her haste. He watched her settle herself full length before the fire, the liver guarded by her outstretched paws.

He sat before his food and said, "I didn't mean to lie."

"I know, Amant," said the Mistress gently. "Emrack knows it, too." She began to eat her stew.

"Does he? I think he would rather I was a liar."

The Mistress sighed. "You must understand . . . Emrack has believed his nephew to be dead." A look of concentration clouded her expression. "He worries, too—for Osei, who is not well; for what is left of the Academe, poor as it may be." She smiled. "This is not what your Ebster taught you to expect, is it? You came to Kheon seeking an Academe filled with eager chanters, all serious, full of talent, each ready to become the greatest orphic there ever was since the day wild Aenan lifted his voice to song! Instead, you find a nearly empty house, a garden gone to seed, one crazy man, one odd woman, and your cousin, whom you hardly expected to find here. Strange for you, I daresay."

Amant nodded, although he barely heard what she had said, because he was thinking and wondering. "My uncle?" he said almost whispering. "Emrack is Osei's father?"

"Emrack Lizatial, a fine orphic. Your uncle, yes," she said. She ladled out a second helping of the stew for herself and watched the teka. The animal had finished off the liver; she jumped up into the chair that Emrack had left and curled herself onto the cushion.

"I don't believe it," said the boy, at last. "Why is

Osei here? How did she come here and why? What is wrong with her? How . . ."

"Please," said the Mistress. "Please. I will answer your questions—but not now. I'm too tired to begin an explanation. I think you must be too tired to listen. Can you trust me when I say I will answer your questions later? Please. I do know how hard it is, to have questions and no answers. But I promise, I will answer them."

Amant could not say no to the Mistress, because she was right—he was quite tired. So, he nodded. But he was uneasy. Glancing at the door of the kitchen, he said, "I can wait, but I don't think the orphic Emrack would want me to stay. He . . ."

The Mistress shook her head. "I will speak with him, before the day is over. Trust me. Here— eat." She nodded at his untouched meal. "You must be as hungry as your wild little pup."

Amant began to eat. *What else can I do?* he wondered. He did not wish to leave without speaking to Osei again.

The woman with the pale eyes sat down next to him and asked, "What name do you call yourself?"

He glanced up at her and smiled thinly. "It seems that I have many names—but which is true?" He shrugged.

"Which do you choose?"

"I? I . . . would say Amant."

"Why?" asked the woman. "A moment ago, you called yourself a very long and strange name— one I have never heard of. How did you say it? Nowaetnawidif . . . who gave you . . ."

"Amant Wuulf-Moas is my Kielding name," he said, ignoring her question. "Why do you call yourself the Mistress of the Academe, if there is no more Academe?"

She gave a low chuckle. "Amarra Nie is my Kielding name," she said. "We have similar names, eh, little brother?"

Startled by her teasing familiarity—and by how she had avoided his query as neatly as he had avoided hers—he laughed heartily.

She smiled and then pointed at the teka, who had fallen asleep in the chair. "Tell me," she said, "what do you call your fierce companion?"

"Hmm? Why, I don't call her anything. I haven't given her a name."

"Well, perhaps you should ask her!"

"Ask?" He shook his head, thinking the woman silly. "How can I ask her? Show me."

He thought the Mistress was teasing him still, but to his surprise he saw she had become serious.

She said, "All things have a name. It is up to you to uncover hers, if she has not let you know it yet."

Amant said nothing to this. He stared over at the sleeping animal. He thought that what Amarra Nie said was odd and yet, somehow, also true. He remembered how Chanutiallin Lo Dianti had once told him that, although the steppes looked lifeless and empty, every bush had a name; behind each blade of tough grass lay a desert creature, and all of these had names; and if he looked hard enough, he would know that the very pebbles had names. . . .

Amarra Nie stood up and put her dish in the water trough. She said, "I think we could both use some more sleep." She leaned over and tapped her fingertip on his bowl. "Finish and I will take you to the chanter's nook. It has been empty a long time, but I think you will find it comfortable."

He nodded and tilted the bowl to his mouth. He was tired—exhausted. He felt it a chore to eat the rest of the stew and then even more difficult to follow the Mistress upstairs, past the room where the translucent bells stood, past the room where he had seen Osei, into a long room at the very end of a second hall, which adjoined the first. This place—the chanter's nook—housed nine beds in a row. Each bed was exactly the same, with a pillow and a dark gray blanket. The beds were low to the floor, set upon bedstands of short, stubby legs. He put his satchel down against one of these beds. The teka hopped up onto the gray blanket, stretching out in the very center of it.

"Someone will wake you," said Amarra. "Later. Sleep well." She lit the wick of an oil lamp set on the wall and left him, closing the door behind her.

Amant undressed quickly. It was cold in the room, and every movement he made echoed in the emptiness. He wondered again what had happened to the Academe to make it so abandoned! He wondered again what illness Osei had gotten, and he was amazed at the strangeness of finding her—and Emrack—here, in the Academe. Everything was a puzzle! And he knew that, no matter how much he thought on it, he would not be able to sort out the pieces alone. The Mistress would have to answer his questions.

He opened the tiny window at the far end of the nook and sat on the edge of the bed he had chosen, rubbing the teka's flat head with his thumb, ruffling her neck ruff of silvery fur with his fingers. *At least we are safe for now,* he thought and smiled. Aloud, he said, "Well? What is your name?" Feeling childish, he stared down at the creature.

She stared back at him and yawned.

"Is your name something simple—or something difficult?" he asked. He stroked her head again, and then said, teasingly, "Are you called Raindrop?" He had once heard a little girl in Mossdon crying to her pet, "Raindrop! Raindrop!"

The teka flapped her wings and turned her arched back on him. She began to smooth down the fur on her shoulder with her tongue.

Amant folded his arms across his naked chest. He was chilly, and he wanted to sleep. Shrugging to himself, he got up and put out the light. In the semi-dark of the rain-soaked day, he felt his way back to the bed.

Two beryl green spots—two teka eyes—stared at him from the bed. He got under the blanket and let the teka find a niche for herself against him. He lay still as she padded around, over his legs, across his stomach, to the end of the blanket nd back before she found the perfect nest, in the crook of his knees.

Amant smiled to himself. As he closed his eyes he whispered, "You are a monster and a tease! Shall I name you 'little monster'? Eh?" He wiggled his toes and jiggled his knees—and got the unexpected answer of a nip on his leg.

"Ow!" he cried, sitting up.

The teka leaped off the bed, shaking her wings at him.

Amant lay down again and pulled the blanket

up to his ears, turning his back on the animal. But, after a few moments, she got back up on the bed and repeated her meandering search for the perfect sleeping spot. Soon, she was snuggled back in the crook of his knees. Amant laughed into his pillow. He said, "You want a name that has a bit more dignity than 'monster', I guess." He tried to think of one—but all his unanswered questions kept jumping about his head, like unquiet crickets in a cage. He could not squeeze a suitable name in between the noisome questions. Finally, he turned over and looked at the green teka eyes blinking at him, and he whispered, "Tell me—tell me what your name is!"

Nothing happened. Curious, the teka stole up to his face and sniffed at him, touching her wet nose to his cheek.

Amant turned over again, pulling the teka with him and settling her against his chest. He was about to drift into sleep, when a name did squeeze itself between all the stuff in his head. It was a word from the *Haaimikin Oide,* the name of wild Aenan's teka-companion, who had helped him search for his lost son. The name was "Nykall" and it means, in our language, shadow.

He said, "Nykall?"

The teka, roused again from her sleep, mewled at him. He laughed and pulled the blankets closer about them both. He knew he had been told the right name.

☆

IT WAS dark with night when Amant heard Osei call to him. He heard her calling clearly; he heard her say "Amant" and he sat up. He knew it was nighttime, but he was surprised that he could have slept so long.

"Osei?" he whispered.

There was no answer. He slipped out of bed, careful not to disturb Nykall. In wrinkled shirt and bare feet, he tiptoed across the cold floor and, unlatching the door, into the hall.

He heard rain on the roof, steady and unceasing. Somehow its constancy reassured him. He stood and listened to it, waiting for Osei to appear—or else, to call again.

"Amant?"

The boy turned around. The voice had come from the same place he had found her earlier, the room with the books. He walked toward it, feeling shaky for some reason. His heart did not pound, but it did beat slow and hard, hard enough for him to feel it knocking against his throat. Or so it seemed. He swallowed and walked onward, not so much afraid as excited and curious. Everyone else slept, he knew—the old orphic, Emrack, the Mistress, Amarra. Even the villa itself seemed to sleep. Only he and Osei were awake, and it was a secret— just as they had once kept their music and their games a secret from their parents, when they were children together in Bildron.

He went into the room of the books, toeing quietly onto the rug. Here, the rain sounded louder. Osei stood beside the window in a white nightdress that hung from her shoulders to the floor, covering her feet. She beckoned him to the window, and, touching the glass, pointed down into the courtyard.

He looked to where she pointed. It was night

again, and the rain fell fast. Curiously, the wishing stone could be seen. It seemed . . . it seemed to be shining, as if a soft light were emanating from within. Amant thought this a very queer thing. He wished it would stop . . . glowing, or whatever it was doing. He wished the stone would be invisible, as it should have been.

"They will come, tonight," Osei said, more to herself than to Amant. "I wish . . . I wish I weren't so afraid. I wish I could go down there and tell them I had made up my mind."

"Who is coming, Osei? What are you afraid of?"

"If only I could go down to the wishing stone . . . but I can't. I can't. . . ."

"But . . ." said Amant, confused. "I saw you, I mean, we met down there, by the wishing stone. We played together, you and I. . . ."

She turned to stare at him. She looked at him for so long without saying anything and with such a surprised expression that he began to doubt what had happened. He said, "I must have been dreaming, again. But it seemed so real. I played ball with someone! Wasn't it you?"

"No."

"Is there . . . is there another girl here, a little girl who looks like you? I met a child in the court-yard, and we played with a big ball. I thought at first it was you, because her face . . . but then, she really was a little child, all bundled up in winter clothes and . . ."

"No!" said Osei. "No . . . she's dead. She's gone!"

"What?" Amant touched his sister-cousin's shoulder. "Who? Osei . . ."

She did not answer him, but shook her head

and leaned against the window-glass, staring at the yard.

"Osei . . ." he said again.

She turned to him. "Will you play with me?"

"What—now?" he said. "So late? Shouldn't you be in bed? And, Osei, who . . ."

"Please play with me."

"It is too late to play games," he said. He was worried for her illness, whatever it was, and he was worried that Emrack would hear them and find Osei out of bed in the cold.

She pouted. "You've grown old," she said. "You sound just like *her*." She glanced at the door and then back out the window.

"Osei . . ." he said.

She smiled at him and took his hand. She was so cold that he put his arm around her to warm her. He was about to ask her some of the questions he had not been able to ask the Mistress, when she said, "I'd like to play ball again. Down in the courtyard, like before. Come with me, won't you?"

Amant shook his head. "I thought you said the girl I played with earlier wasn't you."

She giggled and hugged him around his waist. "I'd forgotten, that's all."

Disturbed, Amant stroked her curly hair. "I think not, Osei. I think we shouldn't go out there, and I think I should take you back to your bed."

"No!"

"Please. . . ."

"No." She folded her arms tight against the bodice of her shift and hung her head, hiding her face from him. And he did not try to bring her out of her hiding by a touch or with words. He felt that something was wrong—very wrong. She could not have simply forgotten their play, nor her fear of the teka. There was *dowanaten* at work in this, too. He had seen a child wrapped in those winter clothes, not a young woman, not she who stood beside him now.

"I have to go back," said Osei suddenly. "Now, I have to go back." She tucked a corner of her nightdress into her hand and pulled the hem up off the floor, so that she would not trip. She said, "Will you come play with me tomorrow night instead?"

"Tomorrow? I will—if Emrack lets me stay here. I am not sure he wants me to stay. I might have to climb over the wall. . . ."

"You can stay. I'll tell him so. Now—promise to meet me here tomorrow night?"

"Why not the morning . . . after you've slept. . . ."

"Here, right here, tomorrow night," she said. "It will be our secret—yours and mine. Don't tell them, because they don't like me to wander about. . . ."

"Because you are ill!" he said. "Maybe you shouldn't. You'll only get worse and . . ."

"I'm not sick," she said. "Not really."

"But . . ."

She touched her fingers to her lips and shook her head. "Please, Amant? I'm so alone all the time, and I can't do anything much. I'm lonely and alone all the long day, while I know that somewhere the sun shines merry and the birds sing. And O! I do remember what it was to be alive. . . ." She began to cry, the tears squeezing out of her eyes and running down her cheeks.

Alarmed, Amant hurried to her and held her close. He promised he would come to her, whenever she said.

Hand in hand, they stole out of the room, into the hall. The rain had stopped and the moon was out. Its brightness made the shadows on the floor more blue than black. Osei walked with her brother-cousin down to where the two halls intersected. Then she pointed to the door at the very end of the hall. She let go of his hand.

"Tomorrow?" she whispered.

He nodded, and she ran past the chanter's nook lightly. Her bare feet made no sound. He watched her open the final door, pushing on it hard. With a wave at him, she went inside.

He stood, undecided. He was cold, but he was not sleepy. Not after sleeping all day. He thought he might get himself a book to read, so he went back to the study. Yet, before he chose one of the volumes, he walked up to the window to see if the wishing stone was still glowing or looking odd, as it had earlier.

In the courtyard, only the moonlight shone. The stone seemed to have died into the night. He was about to return to the shelves when a movement caught his atention. He pressed his nose to the window and leaned against the sill.

Amarra Nie stood in the wet, dark yard. Because she was dressed in black, she was hard to spot. Her long, loose hair drifted around her face. Two silvery earrings winked in the bluish moonlight. She strode to the wishing stone and climbed up onto it, perching herself there as the teka had earlier. And, as she sat, the weird light seeped back into the stone. It glowed again.

She climbed off the stone and stood in front of it with her arms outstretched. She began to sing. He placed his ear against the glass, afraid to open the window and disturb her. But he could not hear what it was that she sang.

Out of the darkness, an owl appeared. It was a large bird; it glided into the yard without a sound, to perch clumsily on the wishing stone. Then, it hopped down onto the mosaic floor.

A second owl, then a third, followed the first. Each soared into the court, circled, and landed on the stone, then hopped to the ground. For a moment, they were still—three large, dark-feathered owls, blinking their disk-eyes and turning their curious heads this way and that. Then they all made a queer motion, rather like a pounce a cat might make upon some quarry. It looked to Amant almost like a dance. Springing upward, they grew, grew, grew, and suddenly there were three women in the yard and no owls.

Amant caught his breath and closed his eyes. *"Dowanaten,"* he whispered. "Not now, not again." He kept his eyes shut for a few minutes, asking wild Aenan to end the haunting. When he opened his eyes, he expected the women and the owls to have vanished. He expected to see only the Mistress, singing a song to herself, by herself, in the yard. He hoped.

He opened his eyes.

The women were still there, all three: a tall, thin woman with ebon skin and silver hair, dressed in yellow; a smaller woman, with sandy hair and tawny skin and a crimson robe; an old woman with auburn-white hair, stoop-shouldered and dressed in cobalt blue. Indeed, the bright clothes they wore reminded him of Osei . . . of a dream he had dreamed in Bildron about her. Had she not worn a strange dress like these women wore, full-sleeved and elegant? Yet, he thought, there was something else naggingly familiar about the women and their clothing, something more than that one particular dream.

Upon seeing these women gathered around the wishing stone in a circle and hearing their voices faintly through the glass as they sang, Amant suddenly knew why they seemed familiar to him. He understood who they were. The boy grew cold, colder even than his sister-cousin, colder than the icy gaze of the Mistress' eyes. Both the *Haaimikin Oide* and the Tales of Kheon speak of such women—have you guessed their names? No?

Some call them the servitors of the Lake Mother; some call them the handmaidens of Trost. Some think that they are evil. Yes, in the West some still think they are evil, but we here know better. They are the daughters of the Lake Mother and the inheritors of her power; old in their ways and gifted with an insight far deeper than even Amant could imagine, they serve as the voice and the hands of the Lake Mother of Gueame. They are beyond all Kieldeans and are more *dowanaten* than any of the most haunted souls in the kith of the *dovai*.

How many of the Tales do you know that mention them? Do you know the story of wild Aenan's death, when the servitors found him lanced through the heart by Death's hand? Do you remember their ministrations to the Lake Mother, when she went mad with her grief? Do you recall that the servitors were granted the gift of youth, to remain young longer than any Kieldean can, to have a life longer than all others? And then, there are the stories about the . . . but, come, I cannot begin to sing every tale, nor tell of all the servitors' powers. It is better to say that Amant had learned to respect the servitors for their *dowanaten*. He had heard the *Haaimikin Oide*'s warning, which goes, "touch not the heart of a servitor's soul; touch not Trost's daughters, nor their kind. Wheresoever they wander, so follows Death behind!" He had seen the frescoes done of the servitors on the walls in the Ebsters' Hall—terrible paintings of tongueless grief and sinister shadows. The Ebsters believed the servitors to be the sole ones in all the world more powerful than they were themselves and thus they despised these daughters, and painted them ill, in those days before the Reconciliation.

Amant leaned forward. Where had the Mistress of the Academe gone? Who was she, to have called forth the servitors from their hidden villa? Why had they come? What did they want? No wonder Osei had been afraid! He had put his hand on the window, craning his neck to see better, when the window's latch came undone and the window flipped open. It whacked against the outside wall.

Amant gasped and lunged toward the window's handle, to pull it shut. The Mistress ran to the middle of the yard and looked up. The other women gathered around her, and for a moment, the boy and the women stared at one another. Then, yanking the window closed, Amant fled.

8
Emrack

LYING HUDDLED ON the hard bed in the chanter's nook, Amant waited for the Mistress of the Academe the others, the servitors, to come for him. He assumed they would chase after him, for spying on their gathering. He pulled the blanket up over his head, although he knew he could not hide, not really. How could anyone hide from the ones who were older than the eldest Ebster, more ancient than the *dovai*'s most revered member? How could Amant hide from those who could make a black wishing stone shine in the dark, as if it were one of the massive lanterns in the Mossdon Kield lighthouse? The servitors could surely see him even now, shivering in his bed!

As he thought these things, his heart sped. Nykall, sensing Amant's unrest, crawled to him and curled up against his stomach. In turn, he curled around the teka. He waited and feared what the servitors might do, when they arrived at his side. Yet, oddly enough, he began to hope that they would come soon, to end the agony of his waiting.

However, he was disappointed in this hope. He waited and waited, but nothing happened. Soon, his heart stopped its frantic dance; his limbs relaxed. He stretched out one leg tentatively. He turned over. He listened, but heard nothing except his own breathing.

He lay for what seemed a long, long time in this position, on his back with the blanket over his head and he thought. What he thought was this: He had run away.

Now, you may say that my great-great-grandfather's thought was a simple one and not so surprising—of course he had run away from the servitors! Wouldn't you? But Amant did not see this as a simple thing. Hiding under the bedclothes in the dark, he thought to himself that he *always* ran away, whenever he was frightened or whenever he did not understand something. This was an unpleasant, startling discovery to him, because he also knew that this running away of his had never once helped him at all. Running away could not show him why he was frightened, nor could it help him understand whatever it was he feared.

Uncomfortable with these thoughts, Amant sighed and turned onto his stomach. He clasped his hands under one cheek. What should he do? he wondered. Should he get out of bed and face the servitors? Was he brave enough? No. He bit his lip and waited.

Nykall crawled up to the boy's face and poked her nose at him. Then she slipped out from beneath the blanket and dropped to the floor. He turned over again.

Not a minute later, it seemed, the creature returned to the bed, to mewl and paw at him. He
supposed that she was hungry. He pulled the blankets off him.

"What?" he said, aloud, to the teka.

She mewled.

"What?" He turned over, annoyed. But even as
he spoke, he saw that he and Nykall were not
alone in the chanter's nook anymore.

Emrack was sitting on a nearby bed. He had his
legs crossed and his long-fingered hands folded
on one knee.

Amant froze. He had not heard the man come
in the room—no footsteps, no door latch lifting,
no squeak of bed withes as he sat down. How . . . ?

Emrack said, "Breakfast waits us downstairs. Will
you come?"

Amant sat up slowly. He asked, "Have you been
waiting long?"

The man shrugged. "Not long. But you slept so
soundly, I hated to wake you."

Amant rubbed his face, astonished. He did not
feel as if he had slept at all! He stood up.

The teka, disturbed from her comfortable spot,
jumped out from the tangled blankets. She began
to wash her steely-gray ruff with a few quick licks.

Emrack watched the animal, while the boy picked
up his trousers from the floor and dressed. He
felt groggy. His eyes were puffy and stinging. As
he tied the strings on his pants, he glanced at his
satchel, wondering whether he would be allowed
to stay at the Academe. After what he had been
witness to in the night, he wondered whether he
wanted to stay. Having a touch of wild Aenan's

power himself was hard enough to bear, but to be near the servitors of Trost? He had not bargained for such a terrible thing. Maybe he would sneak into Osei's room tonight and carry her out, take her to a brigantine bound for the islands. There he would nurse her himself. But that meant running away again! He shook his head slightly.

Emrack coughed and stood up. He moved away from the bed, eyeing the teka. She had stalked up to the man and was shaking her wings at him.

"Nykall!" said the boy, testing out the name he had found for the creature.

The teka folded up her wings, clamping them neatly to her flanks. She turned her arched back on the orphic, waved her tail once, and sat down at the boy's feet.

Emrack said nothing. He eyed the creature again and then looked at the boy. Amant was embarrassed. His embarrassment made him clumsy. He had trouble buttoning his shirt properly. He had decided he must say something, anything, to divert the man's scrutiny, when Emrack said, "Oeta sent you to the Academe as his nephew; he must believe he taught you well."

"He was a fine teacher. None better in Mossdon," said Amant.

"And would you study here, with your teacher's friend?" asked the orphic. He clasped his hands behind his back. "I can show you such music as the Ebsters have never known!"

Wary, Amant said, "I don't know that I should stay here. I saw ... I ... Oeta told me that his friend had surely died."

"And Giolla told me that our nephew had surely

died. So we both have been suffering from false-hoods."

Amant stared at the man, trying to understand him by his expression. But Emrack's face seemed like a mask—smoothed of unease, dark, without a sign of pleasure or displeasure. The boy picked up the teka and rubbed her chin. He said, "There are no students here. You told me that there was no more Academe."

Emrack sighed. "Yes. No chanters have sung here for many a seasonchange. I have been . . . too ill to seek them out. But I am still a teacher. Oeta would have told you his friend was worth your time?"

Amant felt he was being teased. Of course Oeta had been full of praise for his younger friend, Emrack! Stubbornly, the boy said, "Ebster Oeta told me his friend had died."

Emrack laughed. "Well, I am not dead. At least, not yet. So, will you stay? Will you stay and help make the Academe something of a school again?" Emrack's manner suggested that he did not care particularly what the answer might be, but his tone and his question betrayed the tension of a wish that Amant would say yes. The orphic walked to the door of the chanter's nook, his long, light jacket billowing behind him. He put his fingertips on the latch and said, "It will be good, having music here again. I have not had a chanter as pupil since Osei and I became ill."

"What is wrong with her? How . . ." asked Amant. He blushed at his own boldness, but persisted in his questions. "Why are there no students here?"

Emrack turned. "I found no one worthy. Many

youngsters take up song-making, but none respect the old training."

That did not answer all his questions. Amant was annoyed. "How do you know that I will be worthy enough for you, when you haven't even heard me play?" he asked.

Emrack frowned and pursed his lips. "Oeta sends you to me as his nephew, and also with his highest regards—do I need more to tell me what your skill is?" He folded his arms. "Perhaps so," he mused. "Come, then. After breakfast, you will play for me, and then I will decide." He picked up Amant's satchel and held it out to the boy, who took it from him. Then he pushed the door open. The teka scrambled out of the chanter's nook past Emrack's ankles.

Amant followed the orphic downstairs to the kitchen, rubbing his face with both hands, trying to wake up. He walked behind Emrack haltingly, half-wishing he might refuse to play for the man and half-wishing to play so well as to put Emrack to shame. Then, too, there was the problem of the Mistress of the Academe. Had she spoken to this orphic-who-was-his-uncle? What had she told him about the servitors and his spying?

Amant expected to find the Mistress waiting for them in the kitchen, but she was not there. As Emrack poured out cacao, divided the blade-seed bread, and cleaned apricots for the eating, Amant expected the Mistress to appear. Finally, he could not abide the silence and the waiting one moment more and said, "Where is the Mistress?"

Emrack sliced off a chunk of blade-seed bread and wrapped the loaf in cheesecloth. He said,

"She had to go visiting unexpectedly. She will come home . . . tonight."

"Visiting? Who?" said Amant.

"She will be back tonight," said the orphic again. He began to eat his meal. "Sit. Have your breakfast."

The boy did as he was bidden. Between bites, he asked, "May I see Osei?"

"No."

"No?"

"She sleeps in the day. She isn't well."

"What is wrong with her—won't you tell me?"

At this question, Emrack's face seemed almost to wither with the sadness it bore. He pulled on his nose and closed his eyes, then rubbed his chin, thinking. He shook his head. "To answer you properly would take a long time and . . ." He sighed.

"And?" prompted the boy.

"And I think we shall wait until Amarra returns to speak of it. Now I have much work to be done— and I would hear you play for me, young chanter. Hurry."

Frustrated but silent, Amant finished his breakfast. Afterward, he accompanied the orphic from the kitchen to another room at the end of the hall, near the stairs. This place was spare in furnishings, nearly as empty as the chanter's nook, yet warmer. There was a cot in it and a table that was littered with staved paper. A great deal of that paper was blank. An ink pot with clawed legs stood on a blotter along with a wooden pen, its nib darkened with dry ink.

Emrack sat at the table and picked up a viola. He tuned it, as the boy watched him. The viola, Amant saw, was an old instrument, far older than any he had been privileged to hold. He could tell its age from the design: the curled-under head, carved pegs, half-moons. . . .

Without a word, Emrack began to play a short and common air, one that every chanter learns early in their lives. Amant had heard it many a time, some renditions superb and some mangled. Yet as Emrack played, he made the air seem new-born, delicate in phrasing, each movement as clear and satisfying to the ear as spring water is to thirst. Emrack played with such skill that the boy's eyes teared with envy and joy. He had heard many orphics at the Ebsters' Hall, but Emrack made them all seem as boys not yet ready for the choir.

When Emrack was finished and bid Amant to play, the boy was so nervous that sweat started under his arms; his fingers shook as he opened his viola's case. Seeing his fingers tremble, he grew angry with himself for being so easily intimidated. He steadied his hands. Lifting the viola from its case, he rested it under his chin and tuned it, keeping his gaze firmly on the tuning pegs and his mind on the tonality of his strings, trying to ignore the man whom he must please. He did hear Emrack shift in his chair and walk over to the window. But, after that, the boy was able to give himself entirely to the strings he played and the song he would make.

He began with another common air, a companion to the one Emrack had chosen. He soon discovered that the pads of his fingertips had grown more tender than he liked, from three days of rest. It irked him so, that he pushed himself to play a more complicated piece for his second song—a piece written by Oeta for the spring fest of Mossdon, and consecrated to the patron of Amant's heart, wild Aenan. He had trouble finishing the piece because his fingers were sore. When he stopped playing, he found that he had been holding his breath, as if even breathing would have disturbed the rhythm.

Emrack said nothing. He did not move from the window. In the light of the sun, his dark face seemed suddenly old, as if the light or perhaps the music had aged him. Then, he said, "Now, play for me one you have written yourself. I recognize Oeta's hand, so beware. One of your own, that he has not touched."

Amant stared at his viola. What could he play that Oeta had not in some way helped him make? He was at a loss. Those songs he had not shown his teacher he felt too meager to give Emrack; everything else Oeta had added to in some fashion, except . . .

"I have one song," he said to the man. "But it is not finished, yet. I have only the beginning. . . ."

"Play," said the orphic.

Amant fitted his instrument to his chin and tuned it again, in preparation for the melody that he had first made in the porter's lodge of Bildron Kield, his childhood song come back to him. He wished that he had a flautist—or two—to accompany him, to complete the song. Indeed, he ardently wished the song were more complete that he might truly impress his stern judge. He wiped his brow on his sleeve and began.

As he played, he let his heart go free, as he had done that afternoon on the road to Kheon when he had played for the crickets. His soul flitted out from him, borne on the music, out and beyond the stone walls of the Academe, away from the Kield's crowded streets, and into the land of a thousand lakes. He soared in his heart past the tilled fields, skimmed the lakes and sported with their leaping fish, spun and tilted with the lake gillians on their migratory jaunt; over the snow-capped mountains he went, and into the desert steppes, the Tenebrian, to hear the ringing winds of the *dovai* and taste their steel once more. . . .

"Enough!" cried Emrack, cutting the boy's song off in mid-phrase. He half-turned from the window, his hands once again clasped behind his back. "Fine," he said. "We begin tomorrow. You have a lot to learn, I see." And with that last statement, the orphic quitted the room, leaving behind one very astonished boy.

Indeed, so astonished was Amant that he did not move from his seat for a few moments. Then, finally, he lifted the bow from the viola and put the instrument back in its case.

Had he not played well? Did Emrack think him too raw? He rubbed his thumb across his tender fingertips and licked his lips nervously. Oeta had warned him that the Academe would be difficult for him. If only his teacher could have known how difficult and strange it was! He wondered if he could learn anything from such a harsh person as Emrack—how could he learn anything if he were always judged lacking, if he were continually tasked with unkindness?

He went up to the window where Emrack had stood, and looked out. The sun struggled to free itself from haze. Thunderheads threatened from a distant hillside. Directly below the window lay a field; beyond it only the sky, because the land dropped off to the sea. There was no Kield wall here because the cliffs formed an effective barrier to any intruder. Amant opened the window and climbed out. He jumped from the low sill to the grass, landed, rolled, and then sat in the damp sweet-smelling hay. Broken stalks of the grass clung to his clothes and hair. He clasped his arms around his knees and whistled a hunting song, one his eldest *dovai*-sister used to sing to hypnotize desert groundling birds and make them easy prey for her lance.

Brushing the grass from his vest at last, Amant stood and walked toward the sky. He waded waist-high in the field toward the cliffs, leaving a swath of wet, matted grass behind him, until he reached the edge of the world. The earth dropped off at his feet and plummeted into the White Sea.

The wind was stiff and cold with winter's breath. It staggered him, gusting and then moaning in a voice that bespoke age. He sat down to listen and to stare at the sea, so far below and quiet-seeming. Near the beaches, the water was clear, sky-blue, but farther out it turned as black as ink, or as a sea gillian's wing. Some paces up from the sand, at the cove's middle, he saw a villa, perhaps the largest villa he had ever seen, built entirely of weathered gray stone. There was, he discovered, a tiny switchback path that led from his perch to the semicircular, pebbled beach. In fact there were several such paths; except for those narrow trails, the beach was inaccessible, hemmed in by boul-

ders. He breathed deeply of the salt air and wondered who lived in the villa and why they had
chosen a spot so far from the protective arms of
the Kield.

Soon, however, his thoughts turned back to
Emrack and to all that had happened to him since
he had stepped across the threshold of the Academe. Sitting there, outside the walls, buffeted by
the biting winds, he felt sorely lost and tearful.
And so, stubborn, he told himself these things.
That he was a good chanter, worthy of Oeta's
teaching. He could do no better than his best. He
reminded himself of what his teacher had told
him to remember: "You are an orphic already. . . .
If you come to doubt the beauty you are vessel to,
I charge you to remember an old man's words."
Yet, even as Amant repeated this to himself, he
heard again the dulcet, delicate strains of music
that Emrack had made. Phantom notes, flitting
inside his head, told him he was a clumsy bear in
comparison to Emrack's swift-darting blue crown.
Envy made the boy's world dark and hid his own
worth from him.

Amant pulled up a tufted shaft of grass and
chewed on one end. It wasn't fair, he thought, for
Emrack to judge him so harshly. He needed more
training. He had not been given his due share in
Mossdon, despite Oeta's efforts. He was young
yet; he could still learn. Perhaps if he practiced
long hours, worked himself as a driver works a
team of carrier mules, and did not rest, perhaps
he might yet earn the name of orphic!

He fell back on the grass, chewing the stem. His
thoughts drifted to Osei and all the maddening

questions he still had about her. He pushed those
questions aside, because he could not yet come up
with answers. Even so, one thought among all the
others would not go quietly away: had Osei known
that the servitors were to come that night when
she had called him from his bed? How? How well
did she know those terrible, insight-ridden women,
and why did his sister-cousin have the same oddly
colored eyes as the Mistress of the Academe? The
answer to this thought suggested itself—somehow,
Osei was linked to the servitors.

He flipped over onto his stomach and grimaced.
He didn't like this answer one bit. And what of
the Mistress of the Academe? A smile touched his
lips. There was something special about Amarra
Nie; she held an odd delight for him that made
him shiver. There was something about her that
negated his fear of seeing her among the servitors, something that made him trust her. He could
not say what it was, except that he wanted to talk
to her again, to meet her pale, icy eyes and ask
her boldly all the questions she had promised to
answer for him. He sprang up from the grass and
put his hands on his hips. Taking two wide steps,
he brought himself to the edge of the world.

O! he thought, *I will be bold, by the granting of
wild Aenan! I will be a worthy son to both my fathers. If
Amarra does not fear the servitors, then neither shall I!*

Having told himself this, Amant felt as light as
the fluff of a blade plant's pod. He straddled the
edge of the world and began to sing one of the
Tenebrian raiding paeans. He nearly shouted it,
matching the strength of his voice to the wind's
moan. His song soared to reach the highest note,

to hit the screaming pitch that had frightened countless Kieldeans to their core, when his voice snapped. It cracked on this high note so suddenly that it shocked him into silence. And the wind sang on, without him.

He cleared his throat and folded his arms across his chest. He had known that his voice was near to the changing, but he had not expected it. Not really. And the taunt of the jongleurs hopped out of his memory: "Did the Ebsters send you away because you are about to lose your pretty voice?"

Amant stood there at the edge of the world, afraid to sing again. Afraid even to whisper. All his boldness had gone now. He turned and began to walk back to the Kield. As he approached the Academe's window from which he had jumped, he saw Nykall sitting on the sill. She yawned and then leaped down at him, landing at his feet. She licked the toes of his boots. This made him laugh. . . .

But even his laughter cracked a little.

He shook his head and climbed back inside the Academe. Emrack had not returned, so Amant left the room, carrying his viola back to the chanter's nook. He thought to nap because after what felt like no real sleep, in spite of a day and a night, he was so tired that his sight would not clear—his eyes were filming over with exhaustion. He blinked and rubbed them but his eyes would still cloud.

He lay down on his cot, slept, then awoke; no matter which way he turned, no matter how he curled or uncurled himself, he could not find sleep again. His thoughts jumped from place to place, and his body was as restless as blue crowns at nesting time; he was active, flesh and soul. He thought of Emrack, who seemed old one moment, younger the next, and who was Osei's father. He thought of Osei and how she had seemed a little girl bundled in winter clothes and then not so little, a young woman, really, who told him he could not have met a girl in winter clothes and then changed her mind. He thought of his own voice cracking. He thought of the Mistress, who could call the servitors of Trost to her wishing stone. He thought of his own *dowanaten* and wondered of what use it might be and why he had been given it.

Finally, he sat up. He could not stay there any longer. He left the nook, intending to find Emrack. He had to have some of his questions answered. He could not wait for the Mistress to return home from her visiting.

Evening had crept in over the land; the sky outside was dark, and dusk hung in the air. He headed toward the stairs and then stopped, turned around, and looked at the door at the end of the hall—Osei's room. He went up to it, and pushed the door open slowly.

Inside, he saw a cradle tucked into a corner beside a shuttered window. The cradle was canopied in a white netting, and Osei was asleep beneath it. He stepped closer. There was a stool at the cradle's foot, as if someone often sat there, keeping watch. Amant pushed aside the netting and touched her shoulder to wake her. She was so very, very cold to his hand. Surprised, he touched her again, but she did not stir. He leaned down and whispered to her, "Osei . . . Osei?"

She did not wake.

He placed his hand flat on her forehead, then touched her neck. Her flesh was as cool as stone, and he wondered if she . . . had she . . . had she died? He stared at her. Had Death . . . ?

He drew his hand away and was about to cry out for Emrack, when Amarra said, "Don't worry . . . don't worry. She has not gone to the Sea . . . yet."

Amant turned. The Mistress of the Academe stood in the shadowed threshold with Emrack.

Amant said, "Please tell me, what illness has she?" His voice cracked, but he did not care. "Tell me! What . . . what have you done to her?' He found that he was shaking from head to toe.

Amarra strode into the room and put her hands on his shoulders. "Here," she said, "here, Osei is not dead—listen to me. . . ."

He pulled away from the Mistress and leaned over his sister-cousin again. "Why does she not wake?" he whispered, more to himself than to anyone else.

"She will," said Emrack, "but only when the night comes." His voice was thick with grief. He walked in behind the Mistress and sat on the stool at the foot of the cradle. He seemed to move with difficulty; to Amant's eyes he also seemed to have become thinner—like a sturdy elm wracked with sickness or entwined, perhaps, with bold istic vines seeking to squeeze the tree's life out. In fact, so much changed was he that Amant started and stepped away.

Emrack smiled wanly. There was a bitterness in the smile, too, that made the light of his eyes sharp. He said, "Do I look so different, already?"

He pointed to the window. "Wait until the night comes to us!"

Amant was so surprised and puzzled that he said nothing.

The Mistress placed her hands gently on the orphic's arm and stood behind him. "If you will," she said to Amant, "I can answer your questions."

Amant glanced away from Emrack, wondering if the orphic was trying to scare him. He said, "Tell me then—what is wrong with Osei? What does Emrack mean about the night?"

The Mistress of the Academe nodded. "Emrack has told you, I think, that to answer you properly will take a long time?"

Amant nodded.

"It starts," she said, "many seasons ago, on a hidden island, in Woodmill Kield. There . . ."

"The Lake Mother's isle?" said Amant, interrupting the Mistress.

"Yes."

"Last night," he said, troubled, "I saw you. . . ."

"Yes. You saw my family, come to speak with me about Osei. . . ."

"You?" interrupted Amant again. "You are a servitor?"

"Surely," replied Amarra. "I thought, after last night, that you would have guessed."

"I knew I had been witness to the handmaidens of Trost," murmured the young man, "but I didn't hold you to be among them. . . ."

She smiled gently. "I am a servitor, as was my cousin, Giolla."

"Aunt?" said Amant. "Cousin?" He looked to Emrack, and then back to the Mistress. He sat down on the stool by Osei's cradle and said, "The Ebsters speak of the servitors as powerful and horrible. Even Mathisianii said they were to be feared. But Aunt Giolla was not terrible, not in the way that the Ebsters say. And you . . . you're not terrible." He shook his head.

The Mistress laughed, but not unkindly. "There are many tales about the Lake Mother and her servitors. Some are true, some are not, and some are only half-true. As with many a thing in this world. I would say, for instance that you know a thousand stories about wild Aenan that have never been heard in the Ebsters' Hall, nor in most Kields as well. Do you not?"

Amant stared at the Mistress. He held himself very still, wondering just how much she did know about him. He expected her to say more, but it was Emrack who broke the silence by saying, "Why would the boy know about wild Aenan? What have you found out about him, Amarra, that he has not told us?"

"That's for Amant to say," said the Mistress.

Emrack turned his gaze on the boy. "O? What does she mean?"

"I will answer after my questions have been answered," said Amant, piqued by the orphic's tone.

"O ho!" said Amarra gently. "The young chanter is right, Emrack; we owe him answers first. Well. So, Giolla was not terrible as you say, because the servitors are not terrible, as the Ebsters would have us be. Only fear makes the Ebsters silly, fear and many long, slow seasons of pride in their own knowledge. But that is their way, for now; the

Mother knows their wishes, and, in time, they will learn to change. I tell you now, the servitors of Trost are simple people who have been granted a precious gift by the Lake Mother. Yet, they are not alone in the gift. As my grandmother once said, many Kieldeans are so gifted with insight. Even a few of the Ebsters."

"The Ebsters say they are the only ones," said Amant. He felt his face flushing red, and he wondered, did the Mistress know of his *dowanaten? If she is a servitor*, he thought, *she must know. . . .* He said, "But they aren't the only ones, are they? I mean, besides Trost's servitors. . . ."

"No. Still, Kieldeans fear the insight. They have lost any understanding of the gift, and so they let it die within them."

"Does it? Does it die?"

"O, yes," said the Mistress somberly. "But, don't you think discarding such a gift, without exploring it or trying to see what the Lake Mother would have you learn from it, is a thoughtless thing to do?"

"I don't know," mumbled Amant. "Maybe. Maybe it is easier to let it go."

"Easier? Certainly. There are many things that seem easier to do than others. Sometimes it seems easier to lie than to tell the truth; sometimes it seems easier to cheat than to be fair; sometimes it seems easier to steal than to ask. . . ."

"No!" said Amant, standing up. "That isn't what I meant. . . ."

"Isn't it?"

"No. Because . . . because you only hurt yourself, if you lie or cheat or steal." He sat down again, saying, "You only hurt yourself."

"Yes," said the Mistress. "And Giolla did hurt herself. She was never a healthy person. All her life she was sickly, and as a servitor, she had great trouble with the responsibility of her insight. So great was her trouble that she began to drink wine to calm and soothe herself, to help her forget. She drank too much, trying to run away from herself and from the power the Lake Mother had given to her."

Emrack touched the Mistress' arm and said, "She did struggle, though. She tried to do the Mother's bidding." He pulled a chair from a corner and sat down by the cradle. "Giolla and I met here, in Kheon, at the Academe. I was a teacher and she . . . she had come in response to a wish that I had made upon the wishing stone." He gave a short, pained laugh. "That wish should never have been made."

"Hush, now," said the Mistress. "You asked for something many people often ask after. Trost cannot grant it, even though she is bound to answer all wishes and fulfill dreams. It is the only wish that may never be granted, at least not in the way that we understand. Giolla erred in trying to give you your wish without Trost's sanction. As my own mother once erred."

"What did you wish?" said Amant.

"For youth and very long life," said Emrack. "I asked that I might not grow old and lose my beauty and the strength of youth." He sighed. "Such shallow, simple vanity! Vanity, to want youth everlasting."

"Which we are all prey to." said Amarra. "Growing old frightens everyone, Emrack, especially when you are young and youth is good, and you are in love, as Giolla and you were. She, as a servitor, would have outlived you, always younger. She stayed here with Emrack, and tried to answer his wish. But all her entreaties to the Lake Mother were turned aside. Even so, she begged and pleaded. And the seasons passed. She grew bitter with asking. . . ."

"But we made a life together, she and I," said Emrack quietly. "We grew together, and although she would wander from time to time, as a servitor must, she always returned. Except . . ." He shook his head.

Amant frowned, thinking about his aunt. He said, tentatively, "But Osei was born in Bildron. Aunt Giolla lived with us, for as long as I can remember."

Emrack nodded, but said nothing.

"Yes," said Amarra, "Osei was born in Bildron. Giolla left Kheon just before her child was to be born, beause she had slowly, O so slowly, ruined the Academe by her drinking. The debts she incurred took away the school's resources. She had even stolen linganuli from the younger chanters. There was so little left that she panicked. Afraid to tell Emrack what had happened, afraid too for the health of her child, afraid finally that because she could not answer Emrack's wish, he would not love her, she fled the shame and went home to her brother."

"I knew she had been drinking too much," said Emrack. "I knew, but I did not understand how serious it had become. Maybe I didn't want to know. And . . . well, servitors have great powers. Maybe I feared that power in her too much. When she disappeared, I thought she would soon return, as she had always done before. Then, I thought she had gone to the Lake Mother's villa, to rest and be with her family. I didn't worry for awhile, but at last, of course, I did. I went looking for her everywhere, first in Kheon and then all the way to Woodmill, on the shores of Lake Wyessa. I grieved and I searched, but I could not find the Lake Mother's villa nor could I find Giolla. She had never told me about her brother, so I never thought of Bildron. Soon, I believed that I would never see her again, nor ever hold my child in my arms, until the day that I was called to the Sea by Death. I began to ponder death and to look forward to it in a dreadful, despairing way."

"But Giolla did return," said Amarra.

"My . . . my mother said so," murmured Amant, remembering Seftenir's bitter words and sorrow. "My mother said Giolla took Osei and disappeared, after my father died."

Emrack nodded and sighed. His face seemed leathery in the half-light, and when he looked up, his eyes had lost their shine. "She came home to me, with our daughter. She was very ill, by then, very ill. I scarcely recognized her; her face was swollen and she coughed terribly. I tried to nurse her; I tried to wean her from drinking; but my efforts ended in arguments. And finally, well, my heart was no longer in my nursing. I know this is a cruel thing to say, but it is a true thing, nevertheless. I had more heart for the little, silent girl

Giolla had brought home with her than for her mother, who had become so pitiable. Giolla, I'm sure, could sense my growing estrangement. We scarcely talked. She wouldn't let me help her, even when I tried."

Amarra walked over to Osei's cradle and readjusted the netting. "My family and I, we did not know how serious Giolla's problems were, until very late. They tried to call her home, as the servitors always have called the youngest of them home when the time comes for her to take her place among them, but she did not answer. So my grandmother became very worried, and sent Giolla's mother out after her. But, by the time Parella did arrive in Kheon, Giolla was preparing herself for the Sea of Sansel's Net."

"It was a terrible time," said Emrack. "Giolla was barely conscious, and her mother, Parella, was beside herself with grief and guilt, thinking she might have helped her daughter more, had she known Giolla's weakness better. We paced the hall together, she and I, and spoke of the past. Sometimes, we would sit in the yard, under the winter sun, with Osei, watching her play, and waiting."

"But," said Amarra, "Giolla would not let Death lead her away, not yet, because the wish that Emrack had made as a young man, the wish that had brought her to him, was still unfulfilled, and it haunted Giolla's last days. So, before she would agree to accompany Death to the Sea, she forged an answer for Emrack—a bargain, if you will, with Death."

"How?" said Amant. "What kind of bargain do you make with Death? How can such a thing be possible?" He shook his head, disbelieving. "What is it, this bargain?"

"Giolla, despite her faults, was still a servitor," said Amarra. "She had vowed her life to serving the Mother, and she had been gifted with insight. When Trost would not answer her pleas for Emrack, she turned to Trost's sibling, Death, instead."

"One day," said Emrack, "Giolla gathered what little strength she had left and used her insight to help her find Osei. The child was playing alone in the courtyard. I had gone to chop some wood, and Parella was asleep in the chanter's nook. Osei was surprised to see her mother awake and on her feet. The two of them spoke out there, beside the wishing stone, and two things happened: Giolla pledged her daughter to Trost and gave her the tears that test and strengthen insight, and she pledged Osei to Death also, bargaining for my life and youth."

"I don't understand," said Amant, beside himself with frustration. "How could Aunt pledge Osei? What tears are you talking about? What bargain? . . ."

"Amant," said the Mistress. "Listen, and have some small patience. Osei is, as I am, as Giolla was, a daughter of Trost, a servitor's daughter. Most of us are pledged by our mothers, from the time we are very small, to the service of the Mother, if we are gifted with insight from birth. The tears that Emrack speaks of are Trost's most special gift to her daughters, which greatly strengthen such insight as they have been granted. It is not an easy thing to bear, Trost's power, and so most of us are taught early what responsibility lies before us. Giolla had been instructing Osei, but haphazardly; and when she became ill, she knew she would have to hurry her daughter along."

Amant felt his head spinning; he had heard many stories about the servitors, as the Mistress had said, but not this one. He knew it must be true; he knew his sister-cousin had always been connected to his *dowanaten*, but he had never considered the fact that she might be *dowanaten* as much as he was. He looked down at Osei again and whispered, "What bargain did Aunt make with Death?"

"As you see," said Emrack. He stood up and stepped closer to Amant. His shoulders were as sunken as his eyes, which had receded into his skull, as if they had seen too much wickedness and would hide if they could from the world. He looked a wraith, and, as he pointed again to the window, his hand shook as much as a bird's fluttering wing. "During the day," he said, "Osei belongs to Death. She must stay on the Shore of Sansel's Net and minister to the souls of those who have joined the Sea. She gives comfort to those who cannot join and, when her sister servitors bring new souls there, Osei greets them. I am, during the day, lent her vigor and her health. For you see, not long after Giolla died, I too became ill, with a winter-fever that lingered into summer. Giolla's bargain with Death was that I could not die—ever, or at least not so long as Osei was alive to be Death's handmaid and to lend me her life. During the night, I take back my illness and become as near to Death as a man can get without dying. That is when Osei is free again to come back to the living world. Still, it is a narrow freedom. She roams only this house, only during the quietest hours, when all the world sleeps. For a time, in the early evenings, we can speak together, a father and daughter—during the change from day to night. But then, I become too ill for speaking. Poor child . . . she is so lonely, and Death is a jealous master." He sat back down on the stool and wept quietly, his face averted from Amant. He sounded inconsolable.

The Mistress knelt and held the orphic's hand. Eventually, he half-smiled and said, "Osei will wake soon."

Amarra nodded and looked to Amant. "Ever since my grandmother sent me here," she said, "I have tried, by the Mother's granting, to end this bargain. I have gone so far as to have spoken with Death myself. After you saw me last night, I left this world, with the help of my sisters, and made a journey to the Shore. But although Emrack has offered himself to Death, although he has called back his wish, Osei will not agree to come out from under Death's shadow."

"Will not?" said Amant. "Or cannot?"

"Will not," replied the Mistress.

"Amarra," whispered Emrack. "Please."

The Mistress nodded. She stood and, taking Amant's hand, conducted the reluctant young man into the hall, away from the orphic and Osei. He followed Amarra, tight-lipped with worry and frustration. He wanted to speak with Osei, to hear what she would say for herself about the story he had just heard. When he and the Mistress reached the study, Amant burst out, "Why will Osei not end this bargain? Why? Why have we left them? I want to speak to my cousin when she wakes."

The Mistress sighed as she paced up and down the rug beside the floor cushion. She said, "Osei is stubborn and frightened. She will not consent to her father's dying. If ending Giolla's bargain means that Emrack must go to the Sea with Death, Osei will not leave the Shore. Her stubbornness grieves me, nay, cuts my heart and Emrack's too. Still, I understand. It's a grim choice she must make, and she is still very young in the ways of her insight."

Amant lingered at the threshold of the study. He glanced into the hall anxiously and said again, "Why have we left them? I must speak with Osei."

"Shut the door and come over here," said Amarra.

Startled by her abrupt order, so different from her usually gentle tone, Amant did as she had asked. "Why . . ." he began.

"Because I would allow father and daughter some small time to themselves," she said sternly. "Emrack is the only person, I think, who might really help Osei make the decision she must make. And because I want to talk to you, where Emrack cannot listen. Last night, when I spoke with Death, I discovered that Osei had asked if her soul might not be forfeit so that her life could be given entirely to her father." Amarra sat down and rubbed her upper arms briskly, as if she had felt a cold draft. "Do you understand what I am saying?"

Amant stared at the Mistress. He opened his mouth to speak, caught his breath instead, and closed his mouth. At last he whispered, "Has Death accepted Osei's request? Is she . . . is she going to die?"

"No," said Amarra. "Not yet." She tucked her feet under her. "She would have to give up her insight, give up being a servitor and go into the Sea, as all souls do. She is not ready to relinquish that which the Lake Mother has only begun to teach her. Osei is caught between two worlds and two pledges." The Mistress ran her hands through her hair. "Tell me, when you saw Osei in the courtyard, what did she say? How did you find her?"

Amant did not hear the question. He was thinking of his dream, where Osei had refused his help, had refused the broth he would have had her take, and had pushed him away. He remembered too how she had beckoned him toward the sea in his *dowanaten*-dream, how she had seemed to want to drown and to drown him with her, and how he had heard Amarra's voice calling him back to life. He hugged himself with worry and said, "So, if Death has not accepted Osei's wish, how can we save her? Can't the Lake Mother help? Can't you just . . ."

"Amant," said the Mistress. "When you saw Osei in the courtyard, by the wishing stone? What did she say?"

"What? O . . . yes. I *did* see her, in the courtyard. Emrack thought I was lying when I said I saw her there."

"Yes. But I know you weren't lying. What did she say? How did she look? What was she doing?"

"It was strange," he said. "She was so little—a little girl. But I thought . . . she looked like Osei, the Osei I remembered. She was playing ball out there by herself and she wanted me to play with her." He frowned. "She didn't say anything."

Amarra was frowning too. She bit her lower lip and seemed as if she was holding back tears.

Amant said, "It was strange—because Osei later told me she had not played a game with me in the courtyard. I thought then that I had been *dow* . . . dreaming." He folded his arms, unsure as to whether the Mistress could understand what he meant by *dowanaten*. He thought she would; she was a servitor, she would understand. But he was afraid.

She said, "You must try to find that little girl again, Amant. You must try to make her speak to you. Use your insight and call her out of the past. You did see Osei; you saw her as she was before Giolla gave her the tears of Trost and pledged her doubly."

"Only servitors have insight," he said.

Amarra rubbed her forehead and frowned at him again. "You know that isn't true."

"The Ebsters say . . ."

"Amant."

He turned away from the Mistress' keen but gentle glance. He wished he had never heard of the insight or the *dowanaten*. He could not use it in Gueame; he could never be a servitor or an Ebster or a warrior, like wild Aenan; so of what use would the power be?

"You must use it," said Amarra, as if she could hear his thoughts, "to find little Osei again and try to convince her that she ought to help herself choose life. She has to take the responsibility herself and choose between Death and life." The Mistress slapped her open hand against her knee. "She must see that her life, as a gift from Trost, should be lived! It's not right for her to linger on the Shore; it's not right that such a young child, with so much to give this world, should go to the Sea before her time. I love Emrack, fully as much as Osei does; I don't wish to lose him, but he is ready to go. Osei knows it, in some part of her soul. She knows the choice she must make—the choice to live."

"Yes, I know," said Osei. She stood in the doorway.

"Osei!" cried Amant. He stepped toward her.

But the young woman did not heed him. She stared at the Mistress and said, "Yes, I know what you want me to do. You want me to do as you have done, Snow-Eyes. You would not save your own father's life—your name should be Snow-Heart!"

Amarra stood up. "That . . . that is cruel, child. And it is wrong. It is wrong to keep Death from those who belong. . . ."

"Cruel? Who has been cruel? Why did you come here, to worry me and my father? Why didn't you stay away!"

"I came at the Mother's bidding, as you know full well," said Amarra quietly.

"You're a coward," said Osei. She spoke with such vehemence that Amant half-turned toward the Mistress, as if to offer her protection from his cousin's words. But Amarra did not seem in need of protection, nor did she seem particularly angry. Her face wore an expression of sadness and pain.

Osei turned to him and said, "She would not offer her life for her father's, as I offer mine! That is why she says such things about me. That's why she wants to confuse me."

"That isn't true," said the Mistress.

"Isn't it? Isn't it? Your mother told me, Snow-Eyes. She told me how you had turned away Death's embrace when it would have saved your father's life."

"My mother . . ." said Amarra. "My mother has not been well, as you know, Osei. I do not believe she told you I had done the wrong thing by denying Death."

The young woman shook her head. She was crying, furious tears. "Oh, no, no, she never said you had done the wrong thing. *I* say that. I know."

"Do you?"

"Osei . . ." said Amant. He stepped closer to her, wanting to hug her, to help in her in some way.

"I know! I do!" she cried.

"Osei," said Amarra. Her voice was calm, but she appeared shaken. "Your father does not want your sacrifice."

The young woman hurried over to her brother-cousin and took his hands in her own. "Help me," she said. "You must help me. Come with me to the wishing stone, and I will show Trost how deep-rooted my wish is."

"If your desire is so deep," said Amarra, "you must go to Trost alone, Osei."

"Please, Amant," begged the girl. She stroked his cheek and put her head against his shoulder. "Please, it's the only way. . . ."

Amant shivered. "What should I do?" he asked himself. "What should I do?" He closed his eyes, so that he would not have to witness Osei's pain, as he broke from her embrace.

"No!" she screamed.

But he was already gone from her. He ran out to the hall, down the stairs two at a time, past the courtyard, into the street. He ran. He ran until he reached the Kield gates, and even then he only hesitated a moment before dashing out of the Kield, unmindful of the porter's puzzled cry. The gates shut behind him. He kept going uphill, up and up, until he was so out of breath that he was forced to slow down and breathe. He veered off the road, then onto the hillside and blindly into the graveyard there.

9

In the Graveyard

MOONLIGHT LIMNED THE gravestones and bleached the golden grass to a pale yellow. Amant wandered and stumbled across the field to a high spot, from which he could see the whole Kield below. He sat, leaned against one of the faceless stones, and looked at the street lights and window lights of Kheon, patterning a constellation come down to the sea's edge. Only then did he think! He had run away again—again!

From the stone against which he sat, something dropped onto his shoulders. He twisted around in fright, thinking of spirits, before he realized that it was Nykall. She clung to him, her hind feet lodged in the folds of his shirt collar. He laughed shakily at his own fear and pulled the creature onto his lap.

"What should I do?" he asked himself aloud, as he stroked the teka and massaged her to sleep. He did not want Osei to die—no! The Mistress was right—Osei should not linger so at Death's side. But he could not wish for Emrack's death, either. He put his chin in his hands and breathed in the

night's clean air. How could anyone make such a
choice? How could he help Osei, when he didn't
know for himself what he would do? He stood,
cradling the teka in his arms.

Down on the road from the Kield, he saw a
shadow move. It marched along the road and
soon resolved itself into a person's form. The person climbed briskly toward the graveyard; it was
the Mistress of the Academe. Amant knew her by
her long hair and firm stride. He stroked the teka
and kept his gaze upon the shadow, until it rounded
a bend and was hidden from him. Still, he waited
for her.

At last, he heard her rustling in the grass. She
said, "Our cousin asks much of us both."

Amant turned to where she stood beside the
headstone and looked up. Her face, paled by the
blue moon's light, seemed hueless and muted, her
eyes as clear as stars. She pulled her hair back into
a thick rope and tossed it over her shoulders. The
silver earrings she wore jingled.

"Our cousin," he echoed. It sounded strange to
him. "I don't know," he said. "I don't know what
to do or how to do anything to help. You say she
must not die. And I don't want to lose her . . . I
couldn't bear it. . . ." he stopped. "But what if she
has chosen? She has that right, doesn't she, to
choose?"

The Mistress sighed. "Yes. I suppose she has
the right to choose for herself. But how can she
decide? Her mother has bound her to an impossible legacy, at an age too young to know much of
the world, or of life. I know, if it were possible,
that she would save her own life and her father's

too. She doesn't want to die, not really. Sometimes I think she is waiting to see if Death won't relent and allow the Lake Mother to fulfill Emrack's long-ago wish. But it cannot be. Even if Death did relent, the Lake Mother would never fulfill the wish."

"No?"

"No." Amarra turned to look at her new-found cousin kindly. "There is no life without death—they are a part of one another, as the Lake Mother is a partner to her sibling, Death. How many of us would wish for life everlasting, out of a fear of Death?"

Amant frowned. "Many."

"Yes. Do you know the story of the mendiri?"

"I . . . yes, I have heard of them."

The Mistress cocked her head. "Then you know that they had found the secret of life everlasting; they stole it from both Death and Trost."

Amant closed his eyes. "It is a terrible story. I remember, every time the Ebsters would tell it, many of the youngest would cry."

Amarra nodded. "Between Death and Trost there is a balance. If Osei chooses to go to the Sea before her time, the balance will be maintained, but at a great cost. The cost of her youth, her talents, what she could give to the world through living. Emrack has shared himself, as the world has shared with him, many seasons. Although I grieve for him, it is time he traveled to the Sea and it is time for his daughter to be in the world. If we lose Osei, much more than one soul will be lost—I fear a little piece of the world's life itself will go out. You know that the secret of life everlasting gave the mendiri no happiness, no joy; indeed, it brought horror to them, such horror that in the end they begged Death for respite . . . so the Tales say. Even as a servitor of Trost, I do not know much of Death's realm. I respect and fear it. Yet, do we not also sometimes fear life?"

Amant nodded and pulled up a sliver of grass. He chewed on the sweet nib and said, "Yes. But when . . . when we lose someone we love, someone we care for and who cares for us, it is so cruel. We grieve—just as the Lake Mother grieved, for her child and for her Aenan."

"You cannot grieve over the past forever, Amant," she said.

He tore up another stalk. "I know."

She sat down beside him and folded the edges of her black robe around her knees. "You have lost many people to Death, for one so young."

Amant swallowed the dryness in his throat and nodded. He did not know how she had found out about his past and about the *dovai*, but as she seemed to know, he said nothing more. He glanced at her swiftly, out of the corner of his eye, and murmured, "Snow-Eyes?"

The Mistress of the Academe started, and she looked at him narrowly.

"Osei called you 'Snow-Eyes'?"

"A childhood name that my father gave to me."

"Is it true, what Osei said about your father? Would you . . . did you refuse?"

"Yes." Amarra put her chin on her knees and stared out across the field. "I refused Death. Because I knew it is wrong to keep people back from the Sea, if it is their time to go. My father knew

this, as Emrack does. My father . . . understood."
She laid back in the grass, clasping her hands
behind her head. For a long, long while—or so it
seemed to Amant—she lay there motionless, with
the moonlight upon her like a veil.

Amant stroked Nykall until the teka shook herself and launched into flight. He watched the creature sail across the star-spread night, and he
thought of the things that the Mistress had said.
He did not look at Amarra; yet, slowly, he became
more and more aware of her presence next to
him. He sensed her near him, as you might feel
the heat of a flame against your skin, though you
were blind to its light. This feeling agitated him so
that his heart sped and his head felt heavy. He
flushed and his face grew hot, from hairline to
neckline. He felt Amarra's presence as a pressure
of him, constricting him, suffocating him almost,
and, finally, he had to do something or he would
explode. Cautiously, as if he were made of glass,
he stole a glance at her.

Amarra had fallen asleep. Her strange, glitter-
ing eyes were hidden behind their deep lids; her
lips were parted and she was smiling, but not
broadly—a secret smile of a dreamer dreaming
well. He found himself drawn to her, almost as a
child's kite is drawn to earth after flight, skittery,
resistant, but captured and drawn down to earth.
She was quiet. He watched her, and watched. And
as he sat there, vigilant over the sleeping Mistress,
the music of that song he had played for Emrack
whispered to him. The deep viola hummed and
the flutes . . . but now, he also heard a singer. A

voice, the fragile soprano of a child's voice, sang to him, and the words he listened to were these:

Fire, my beloved, and I the earth's child
as a forest before the flame, new-made into coal,
as a grassy field, eaten by the igneous demon,
as a young willow, full-leaved, tongued into ash . . .

He stood up quickly, frightened—who was singing? He looked down at Amarra, but she had not stirred. And, as he gazed at her, he found himself leaning down and reaching out. . . . He snatched his hand back and took a step away. His desire to touch the Mistress had grown so strong that he almost *had* touched her. What, he wondered, would he say to her, if he woke her? How could he explain the touch and his feelings? How could he explain the song?

Embarrassed, he walked toward the edge of the field, to where he could see the ocean below. Suddenly, he wanted to take the path to the beach and swim, to wash himself in the frosty waters.

Or better yet, he wanted to soar with Nykall, out over the dark sea, out past the breakers and the lights of the Kield, to where there were only the inky swells and the moon. He put his hands on his hips and watched Nykall hover above him. She tilted and rolled, soaring back across the graveyard as if daring him to catch her. He laughed and took chase. He deliberately spread his arms in imitation of the creature. He dipped his body when she rolled. He copied her antics, spun about and ran, and as he ran he imagined himself becoming a teka. He would test the *dowanaten;* he would dream of launching himself into the sky, to shoot toward the blue moon on black wings. . . .

. . . . The ground slanted at an impossible angle and sank from his feet, as water might drain swiftly from a damaged basin. He lifted his wings in a steady, exultant beat. He flew upward, high, far, far away until he had flown so far above the gravestones that they seemed like pebbles and Amarra seemed like a child's toy and the grass appeared to be as fur on a dogs back. He tucked his arms—his front legs—against his chest and his hind legs flat near his flanks. His sight had altered to a peculiar sort of vision that had no color, but had so much clarity he could see the hills he knew to be distant as clearly as if they were at hand and not in the next Kield.

He spiraled downward as the wind picked up strength. He opened his mouth to shout and wake Amarra, but the sound he made was piercing and shrill, not a human shout but the call of the hunt, "keir-ah!," full of fury.

Nykall answered him. She sped toward him, circling midair. Playfully she chased him, and he eluded her. Never had he felt so free! He hovered and let Nykall catch him. But when she did, a strange thing happened: she gave him a few glancing nips and buffeted him with her front paws. Her ears were flattened to her head and she lashed her tail, moaning in a way he had never heard before. She was not being playful, now.

He dipped and flew from her, toward the field, then landed on the headstone beside the Mistress. She had waked. She sat staring at him, her body rigid. If he had been himself, the young chanter

Amant, he might have giggled at her dazed look. But, being a teka, he had lost laughter. He cocked his head and folded his wings, sitting neatly on the rough, cold stone. A part of him was as stunned at his *dowanaten*-change as the Mistress was. But he felt that part of him fading, as a voice is swallowed in the face of the sea's rumble. The part of him that was Amant was dying and, oddly, he did not care. He would allow the *dowanaten* to be complete; he would not stop the change this time because it was easier to be a teka—so free and wild and without the burden of making choices!

Overhead, he felt Nykall hovering. She began to moan at him again, a low, beckoning mewl that made him jumpy. His stomach clenched. He realized his hunger. He looked up, unfurling his wings and stretching. "Yes, yes," said his new teka's heart, "it is time to hunt." The part of him that was Amant grew ever fainter. He tensed, crouching for a jump into the air.

"Amant!" cried the Mistress of the Academe. "Amant!"

He heard his name. The sound of it, and the sound of the woman's voice were familiar and bothersome. He stopped and glared at the one who had made this noise. He yowled in confusion.

Amarra reached for him. He snapped at her hand. But she was cunning; as he lunged at her again, she caught him by the ruff of fur around his neck. He fought. She got him off the headstone. He kicked and screamed as she dragged him to the ground. Pinning him by her feet, she stroked his flat head and murmured "Amant, Amant," over and over. He felt as if he were being yanked inside out—the tiny, fading part of him that was human came tumbling back from the dark place. His wings and front legs grew into arms, and his tail shrank up into his spine. Shaking his head to clear it, staring at his feet that were once again shod and not clawed, he took a deep breath, a deep breath of relief. He was himself again and glad.

Amarra brushed his hair back off his sweaty face and smiled at him. She was kneeling over him and he was about to speak when her face blanked with pain and then twisted in a scream. She staggered to her feet, turning—Nykall had landed on her back. The Mistress screamed again and vainly tried to dislodge the animal; she staggered from the force of the unexpected blow.

Nykall rose into the air, spun, and dove for another attack, talons extended.

Amant scrambled up and jumped between the animal and her prey. He cried out, "Nykall!" But the teka could not stop. She crashed into him, tearing his shoulder as she scythed by. Yowling, she wheeled and landed in the grass. Her ruff stood out from her pointed face in a silvery haze. She yowled again, watching him and sniffing the air. Then, she loped up to him and cried in a piteous tone, as if to show her confusion.

Stunned, he shouted at the teka, "Get back!" He made a motion as if he might kick her. She retreated, but did not leave.

He helped Amarra sit up. She was breathing hard, in short gasps of pain. "How bad?" she managed to ask.

Amant knelt behind her and gently lifted her

long hair. The robe she wore was slashed, as was the tunic beneath; the torn slits were bloody and her skin scored deeply. He tried to probe the ragged cloth. But she stiffened and gasped, so he let it be and said, "Amarra . . ."

"How bad?"

"You're bleeding, but it's too dark, I can't see. . . ."

"Home," she said. "Back to the Academe . . . must . . . you're bleeding too." She fingered his shoulder gently, where the clothing was tattered.

"Can you walk?" he asked.

"I will. Here. . . ." She grasped his uninjured shoulder and stood. He could feel her shaking with the effort. He circled her waist with his arm, and she leaned against him, and thus they made their way down the hill to the road. He could hear her make a little cry now and then where the road was rough and he misstepped. As the sun rose, he saw her face set with a stubbornness he dared not disturb. Her jaw trembled, and her dark brow was damp.

He said nothing, and they trudged on. His entire side—shoulder, arm, and neck—was throbbing with pain from the teka's blow. His fingers were numb. He felt dizzy and nauseated. He wondered how the Mistress could even stand up, let alone walk.

Fortunately, by the time they reached it, the Kield gate was open and they did not have to disturb the porter. Amant glanced anxiously at the inn and wondered for a moment whether the jongleurs might still be there. Then he remembered that they had said they had a home in

Kheon, and so he dismissed them from his mind. Besides, they saw no one, not even the porter or his brother. The streets were empty, the inn's yard was empty.

Amant and Amarra did not speak. They simply walked. And walked—it seemed forever, to Amant. Only once, when the Mistress faltered, did he speak.

"Here," he said through gritted teeth, "we are almost home."

She made a slight nod and walked on. He strove to keep her standing and moving, although he felt as if he were nearly carrying her. Despite his own failing spirits he did persevere, and he found strength in Amarra's desperate determination. In silence, they reached the door of the Academe.

☆

THE MISTRESS of the Academe kept to her bed. A fever came upon her not a few days after she and Amant made it home, because her wounds became infected and they festered. She lay on her stomach, sometimes asleep, sometimes crying and rocking to and fro from the heat of her illness. By day, Emrack tended her. He changed her bandages and tried to reduce her fever with cool packs and herb teas.

Amant, too, became ill from his wound, but suffered far less than the Mistress. Though he too caught infection from the teka's claws, he recovered quickly and was soon left to himself, once Emrack saw that the shoulder would heal. Much to Amant's surprise, the orphic did not demand to know what had happened that night in the graveyard, nor why. Yet, neither would he tolerate the

teka in the house. No matter that Amant said the
fault had been partly his own; when Nykall returned to the Academe, after three days absence,
Emrack forbade Amant to let the teka inside.

The young chanter felt keenly that he had caused
a terrible thing through his use of the *dowanaten;*
not only was Amarra ill to the point where she did
not even know him if he walked into her room,
but at night Nykall would scratch and whine at the
window of the chanter's nook. It was a forlorn
and lonely sound. Amant felt wretched all the day
and all the night. He took to feeding the teka a
part of his own meal in the courtyard, where he
would sit on the paving stones while she ate and
talk to her as if she might understand. He told her
many things: how he had not meant to misuse the
dowanaten to try to escape the cares of being human; how he had not meant to confuse the teka
and frighten her—he remembered his spiteful kick
at her and was grateful that the kick had been so
ill-aimed. He told her, too, how much he respected
the Mistress, and how he wished he could do
something to help her, and he spoke softly of
Osei, that girl-child Osei, whom he had once met
in the courtyard, all bundled in her winter clothes.
He knew that Osei was caught in his *dowanaten*—or
he was caught in hers, or both—in some way he
did not fully understand.

Most every evening, after Emrack went upstairs
to Osei, Amant would feed Nykall in the yard and
sit with her and talk. Sometimes he played with
her, and sometimes he would bring his viola out
and sing the songs he remembered from the *dovai.*
Now and then he would think about using the

dowanaten again, to try to do as Amarra had asked, to call the little girl out from wherever she was hiding, to find the young Osei and persuade her somehow to come back to life. A few times he almost asked Emrack about the "insight," but he was afraid of the orphic and suspected the man would know nothing more than he, himself, did. There were moments, also, that Amant eyed the wishing stone and thought again that he might ask the Lake Mother to take from him the gift of wild Aenan's power. But he did not act on any of his thoughts. He could not. He knew to whom he really had to talk again—Amarra. So, he wished instead on the wishing stone that the Mistress would be well, and he waited and he sang to her songs of healing from the *dovai*, although he knew she probably could not hear them.

During the days, while Emrack was tending to Amarra's fever, Amant tended to the Academe. As he had once served Oeta's chambers, so now he rose with the sun and made a meal for himself and Emrack. Then, he would practice the viola for the balance of the morning in the empty chanter's nook. The music was always that which he had been taught by Oeta, the rigorous, difficult exercises of the Ebsters' Hall. Some days, he would try to sing, but on these exercises his voice dropped or soared or broke most unpredictably. Then he would stop in frustration. Some days, Emrack would join him, and slowly he began to teach Amant. Yet those teaching days were rare because Amarra continued so ill. Amant spent most of his time alone. He would have liked to help tend Amarra, but Emrack discouraged him. So there was nothing he could do but sing his *dovai* healing songs in the night.

And thus the days passed. Sometimes, in the afternoons, Amant would make another meal and do whatever chores Emrack asked. Then, during the early evenings, before Nykall came to the yard for her supper, he would try to work on the song he had been making since he left Bildron. As soon as he was able after the night of Nykall's attack, he had written out the words he had heard in the graveyard. He remembered the words completely; he even remembered the exact timbre of the ghostly voice he had heard singing those words. . . .

Fire, my beloved, and I the earth's child,
as a forest before the flame, new-made into coal,
as a field of grass, eaten by the igneous demon,
as a young willow in full dress, tongued into ash.

And he added . . .

Fire, my beloved, and I the earth's child,
as fecund acres scorched by thy hunger,
as the brittle conifers made skeletal by thy blaze,
as a bamboo grove, once sweet, is seared by thy lash.

He felt as if there should be one more verse. But he could not imagine it, nor find the words, no matter how hard he tried. So, he left off and took one of the reed flutes he found stored in the chanter's nook and began to teach himself how to play it.

One night, as he was restringing his viola and worrying over Amarra, Osei came and found him.

He had not seen his sister-cousin since the Mistress had been hurt, although he had waited for her in the study at night, as she had asked him to do. Once, he had gone into her cradle during the day, but she had not moved. And once again he had been so shaken by her cold skin and immobility that he had left her.

"Does it hurt much?" she said, startling him. He put the viola and the strings aside and smiled at her as she stood in the doorway, half-hidden behind the door of the nook. She peeked in at him and said again, "Does it hurt much?"

"No," he said as he glanced at the white thatch of gauze covering one shoulder. "It's a little stiff, that's all."

"The Mistress is in pain."

"Y . . . yes. . . ."

Osei sidled into the nook and hopped up on an empty bed. "She meets me now on the Shore. I keep her company, and we've been taking long, long walks there. . . ."

"The Shore," said Amant, his heart heavy and cold. "The Shore of Sansel's Net."

"Yes . . . yes. It is a beautiful place. Don't you remember, I tried to take you there, the first time you came to the Academe. We walked together there, Amant . . ." She shrugged. "Don't you remember?"

"I do," said Amant. He gripped the sides of the bed and swallowed. He remembered a desolate beach and a moaning, empty sea. . . . He remembered a long, flat, gray stretch of land and the bronze light, and he said, "It was not a beautiful place."

"You didn't like it. I know."

"I almost drowned there!"

Osei shook her head. She closed her eyes and sighed. "You didn't like it," she repeated, "but it is beautiful to me, there. I love the Sea."

"The sea is here, too, Osei. Outside these windows and over beyond the cliffs."

She frowned. "You don't understand. The Shore is my home. I belong there."

"It doesn't have to be. It wasn't always your home."

She folded her arms. "I know. You don't understand. I've told you before, I must stay there. I'm going to stay there. And now that Amarra is with me so much, it's no longer so lonely."

Amant caught his breath. "The Mistress . . . is . . . is she going to stay?"

Osei pouted. "I don't know. I hope so, but she doesn't want to."

"Why? Why doesn't she want to?"

Osei shrugged. "The Shore is a beautiful place."

"No," said Amant. "No. Please, Osei. You don't belong there and neither does the Mistress." He stood and walked toward her. "Osei, you must . . ."

She bounced off the bed, eluding him, and darted to the door. "Catch me!" she cried and was gone.

He ran after her. She sped around the corner into the adjoining hall, and he chased her; she ducked into the first room by the stairwell and so he went in after her, calling, "Stop, Osei, stop!" But she did not heed him.

He closed the door and glanced around the room. He had nearly forgotten this place, since the door was never open and he had never thought to ask Emrack or Amarra about it. The bells that had once captivated and surprised him, those bells that he had marvelled at on the very first day he came to the Academe, stood in the middle of the room. Osei sat on one of the cushions arranged in front of the instrument, as if she would be an audience. She was staring at the chimes and did not look away as Amant crept toward her, whispering her name. He expected her to dash off, but she sat still and stared.

Puzzled, he sat down on the pillow next to her. She whispered, "Can you play a song for me?"

"On that?" He pointed at the bells.

She nodded.

"No. I've never seen one before . . . or heard it played. What is it called? Where does it come from?"

"It's called a Ling. My father says it comes from Atrin."

"Atrin?" He stood up and went closer to the instrument. "So far? It must have traveled from ship to ship to get here."

"My father says the trader who gave it to him got it secondhand. Emrack can play it . . . and so could I, before. . . ."

"Show me," said Amant. He ran his hand over the smooth wood, shaped as bullock's horns. He touched one translucent bell and peered at the fine tracery that laced its lip.

Osei came to stand near her brother-cousin. She took up two long sticks that had soft, leather pads on their ends and held them, one in each hand. She said, "To play a Ling, you must first learn well the tone of each chime; then, you tap them, up and down the scale . . . like so." She made a swift motion of tapping, but her sticks did not touch the surface of any chime.

Amant nodded. "You play now—play for me."

"No," she said and her voice was rugged with sadness. "I used to play . . . but now—I can't."

"Can't?" He gently held her by her elbows because she had started to cry. "What is it?"

She shook him off and tapped the chimes with the sounding wands. Nothing happened, no music came from them. Without a word, she handed him the wands. Confused, he touched a bell. Instantly there came a low, full note. It hummed. The hum built to a high ring, and he tapped the chimes lightly, up and down the scale, just to hear the range. The ringing bloomed as the notes sounded and meshed and the chimes vibrated.

Then, to Amant's astonishment, the bells began to change color, their transparency gathering light as muslin would gather dye. Each note produced a different shade; each color meant a separate note. The room thrummed with light and sound. Delighted, Amant played the notes randomly, simply to hear, simply to see. And an arrow of chimelight flew up one of the sounding wands. It grew to an aureole that wavered around him, shifting colors as he played; he was enclosed, joined to the sound. Now and then his hands glimmered with a spark. He stood, enthralled within the flickering halo.

He lifted the wands away from the Ling, and the chimes darkened; silence returned. He sighed and said, "So beautiful." He turned to ask Osei again why she could not play for him, but she was gone.

"Osei?" He hung the wands on the peg from which she had taken them and went out into the hall. It was empty and dark. He quietly walked down to Osei's bedroom and nudged the door open.

She was there, with Emrack. She had crawled into her father's lap and was talking to him in a low voice; from time to time, the old man would answer, but both spoke so softly Amant could not hear. He left them and took himself back to the chanter's nook. He did not wonder anymore why Osei could not play the Ling. He knew somehow that Death had taken this beauty from her, as well as holding her soul captive.

☆

SEASONCHANGE passed, and the winter brought short days and long nights. Each evening, Osei had more and more time to spend with Emrack and Amant; so, each evening, she and her brother-cousin would meet. Amant did not ask her about the Shore, where there was no sunrise and no sunset and no way to mark time because there was no time. He had asked her at first, and tried to make her see the desolation of that place where she lingered in Death's shadow. With words, he tried to convince her to come home. But either she did not respond to him, or else she became angry. So he stopped his talk and let the evenings pass as they would.

And even though he cried outwardly to know how he could help her, in his heart he knew he would have to try the *dowanaten* again, as the Mistress had said. Somehow, Osei might be reached that way. Yet he did not know how and he was afraid. Also, he did not wish to speak about Death because he feared for the Mistress of the Academe. Her fever broke, but she continued ill, and her grievous wounds—for which he felt responsible—healed, but not quickly. He remembered that Osei had said that the Mistress walked with her on the Shore, and he wondered if this meant she too was destined for Death's realm. He grew silent in his fear and perplexity. He let the days and nights go by and did nothing.

Now, one of these winter morns, after Amant had cleaned the dishes and had begun to cook ink for the season as Emrack had asked him to do, he heard, at last, the final verse to the song he had been trying to make. Why the words came to him just then, he did not know, but as he measured out the nutgall and added the arabesque gum, blue coupe rose, and wood chips to water, he hummed the viola part to himself and heard these words:

Rain, my beloved, and I the earth's child,
as desert bunchgrass thrives after thy storm,
as dark loam, stoneles and soft, yields with thee,
as smoke bamboo rustles with thy quenching tears.

Smiling, excited, he lifted the heavy pot of uncooked ink over the fire, to let it boil slowly. Then, he sat at the kitchen table to listen to his whole song sung by the invisible soprano. This voice that sang him the song, it was familiar and sweet and it came from inside him—yet, it sounded outside of him too, as if someone were sitting at his side singing in a whisper into his ear. Someone dear, someone familiar, someone he knew—but who?

Today, the *Song of the Smoke Bamboo* is often sung by choir, at least in the Ebsters' Hall, though it is really too simple for such lavish voice. To me, at least, it sounds better sung as it was meant to be sung—by one clear voice, and a viola and two flutes. It is a simple melody, but not easily forgotten once heard.

Amant sat and listened and smiled as he heard again the ghostly trill of the flutes and the dark viola's sighing. The melody meshed and unmeshed, the words and music twining and then rushing apart and then twining again. He stared into the kitchen's hearth, and the fire there became as the fire in his song, snapping and growing frantic. It became insatiable enough to eat a forest grove, with a roar so intense that he shook his head as if to shake out the sound and the crying of the children, the crying of the desert children, who had thought, at first, that their hearth fires had run crazily rampant, to burn them out of the *dovai*.

But no, it was the corsairs. He saw them again, small people for the most part, smaller at least than his *dovai*-kith, mounted on a collection of animals, some of them mules, some of them scrawny equuilopes. Fierce they were and silent, eerily silent, as they demolished the *dovai*, tearing through its roof and catching the children as they screamed and ran from the intruders.

He had run, too. The tunnels under the winter earth had filled with thick clouds of woodsmoke.

He coughed, suffocating, choking, the smoke drying his throat and lungs, burning his eyes. He crawled with the others to the surface, seeking air, and when the freezing but clear air touched his face, he gulped it down, as a thirsting man would drink at a cool, spring stream. Someone grabbed at him, tugging his elbow, and for a moment he was terribly, terribly confused . . . he thought it was Osei there, in the desert . . . he thought as he looked down through the smoke that little Osei was standing near him, in tears, clutching at his arm for help. He knelt and hugged her, and she whispered that the Kield was on fire, that the raiders had come and they would have to flee, and he promised he would take care of her as all around them the world had gone to ash and the fire ate his Kield, the writhing flames eating the *dovai* from the inside, like a cancer, destroying Bildron, too. . . .

"Amant!" said Emrack. He gave the young man a shake and then stirred the pot of ink. It had been boiling over. He lifted the cauldron off the fire. "It will spoil if you don't stir it," he scolded. He unlatched a window. The kitchen had become dense with the foul odor of the ink-steam.

Amant said nothing, still befuddled by the music's vision.

The orphic sighed, stirred the mess of boiled liquid, and put the pot back over the fire. He dragged a stool up to the hearth, along with a bowl and a basket of purple-eyed berries that needed pitting.

"I will watch the ink," he said. "Why don't you go see Amarra? She is much, much improved, and she was asking after you. Go and visit, when you have finished your practice."

Amant smiled. "She will be all right, then?"

Emrack nodded. "I think, yes." The orphic pointed to the door with a berry-stained finger. "Go and practice! Leave your door open—she would be pleased to hear the music. Go on, she's in the study."

Amant ran off, up to the chanter's nook to get his viola. He resisted peeking in at her as he passed the study on his way to the nook, but he was so excited that he broke a string tuning, and so, after replacing it, he took the music and the instrument and himself to Amarra.

He found the Mistress sitting, propped up on her side by pillows. Her bandaged back was to the door, her face to the window. Sunlight warmed the room and lay in a thick bar over her blankets. There was a fire in the fireplace; she was looking over a book open on the rug beside her.

He walked around her to the window, holding his viola against his chest, as if to hide himself behind it. Although her face was drained of color and thin, she seemed alert and smiled when she saw him. This welcome eased him, and he sat down beside her. He said, "Emrack told me you are better?"

She pushed herself up a little, careful to move slowly. "Much, thanks to you and your music. I heard it, every night."

He blushed and shrugged. "I wasn't hurt so badly—see? I don't need bandages anymore." He pushed aside the collar of his shirt.

"Ah! The marks are nearly gone."

He nodded and glanced shyly at her. "I'm sorry," he said.

She shook her head. "You are not to blame, Amant. A teka protects its own. That is their way. Nykall was . . . confused. She would protect you against me. This is their way. It has been so long since I have been near a teka. I had forgotten their strength."

"You said you raised one—when?"

"I went to the mountains, some time ago," she said. "My brother and sister had died . . . they were older than I, much . . . older. And we had a hard winter." She sighed. She looked down at the rug, but seemed to be staring past its patterns; her eyes had a blank look, half-hooded by their lids. She said, "When my brother and sister went to the Sea, I left my villa, bereaved. I climbed, up and up, to the tiny settlements that cling to Mt. Oron, too small to be called Kields. Up there, I found the teka. Do you know the old, old tale about a Kield made of ice where the mendiri once lived? Have you heard it, in Mossdon?"

"Yes," he said. "It goes, 'High above the desert steppes, and far from the valley's green . . .' "

"Just so," said the Mistress. "But when they tell it, in the mountain villas, they speak of a particular spot, where this ice Kield would be found. Not one of my hosts would go there, because they feared the mendiri. Some said the mendiri still lived; some said their unquiet spirits haunted the place."

"You went by yourself?"

Amarra laughed and tapped his chest with her finger. "Wouldn't you?"

"Of course!"

"Well then," she said. "I was curious. So I climbed."

"And?"

"I found . . . I found a strange villa there. Roofless and half-buried in the snow. It was vast, even if it was falling to pieces. Inside, I found a colony of tekas. They had made the place into their nest. There were twenty of them—eight full-grown and the rest pups. I ran, thinking that they would kill me, but they scarcely bothered to look at me. They were not the killing tekas of Quedahl's children; they were wild and had never seen a person. They let me return, and then, one day, a pup attached itself to me, even as Nykall has done with you. It would not leave me. When I left the snows, my teka stayed beside me."

"Something happened to your teka," said Amant. "What?"

"An accident," she said. "Shipboard. I was sailing from Pacot to Kheon, as a passenger on a spice seller's ketch. One of the sailors got drunk. He decided I needed his company for the night. A firm hand would have taken care of him, I think, but the teka attacked. The sailor defended. His knife was long, and its blade touched her heart." The Mistress winced as she moved, and she sighed. "Take care of Nykall," she said. "She was only doing as her nature bid, protecting you." She paused. "Tell me, what was it like for you to take on the teka's nature? To become one, so completely?"

He glanced away from her keen gaze and began to fuss with his viola.

"Amant," she said, prodding him a little with her foot. "Who taught you to use your insight? Who taught you so well the dream-change?"

He plucked a string. "I don't understand," he mumbled.

"You may not understand my words," she said, "but you know what I mean."

"*Dowanaten*," he said, slowly. "You mean the *dowanaten*."

"What?"

"The power of wild Aenan—you call it insight. My *dovai*-father called it being *dowanaten*."

"Who—Lent?"

"No . . . my father. In the *dovai*."

"Ah!" she said, nodding.

Amant glanced at her and said, "My *dovai*-father was proud of the *dowanaten* in me, because he thought it was a sign that I was favored by wild Aenan. I would have been taught the proper use for this power, if the corsairs had not come." He watched the Mistress gingerly, to see how she would react. He had not really spoken freely of the Tenebrian, or of the *dowanaten*, since the day Oeta had taken him from the slaver's hand. It felt strange to him, to be speaking so. How much should he say? How much did she, as a servitor of the Lake Mother, already know? He waited.

She said, "Tell me about the *dovai*, Amant. What did you learn about the insight there?"

His heart sank. "Don't you know?"

"Know what?"

"Everything! You must—you're a servitor. I thought you would know."

Amarra laughed gently. "Everything? Hardly

that. Sometimes, I wonder if I know anything at all. Insight is a difficult power to bear, Amant, as you have been shown. I have learned some about my own gift, through my grandmothers and Trost's servitude, but I am still learning."

"Still?"

She nodded. "Always. As you will be, always. What did your *dovai*-father teach you, before the corsairs came?"

"Nothing," said Amant, glumly.

"Oh, come. He must have taught you some!"

"Not about the *dowanaten*. If you had not called to me, I would still be a teka. I heard your voice and my name and I remembered myself." He sighed. "I was too young to have learned about the power. So my *dovai*-uncle told me. And now . . . they are gone." He stared at the rug, disconsolate. "I was beginning to hope . . . I hoped you would be able to help me."

"I can."

He glanced up, startled.

She smiled. "I can teach you a little . . . at least, how to stop fearing the power and how to let it work within you. But, Amant, you have learned much already, by yourself. The proper use of the power is a choice you must make. No one can teach you the 'proper' way to understand the insight, except yourself, with the help of wild Aenan, I should think." She touched his arm. "Look to your own heart and trust yourself."

"I don't . . ."

"In music," she said, "When you make a song, whom do you trust? Where does the music come from?"

"I . . ." he began, thinking of the strange soprano who had sung for him the song he had been making, the *Song of the Smoke Bamboo*. He was confused. "I don't know . . . from me, I guess."

"Insight is like music, Amant. A gift from the Lake Mother and wild Aenan, yes, but also a part of you, yourself."

And thus did Amarra 'Snow-Eyes' Nie speak to her cousin of the great and lovely gifts that the Lake Mother—and wild Aenan, although she was less sure of these—had granted to the people of the world. Slowly did my great-great-grandfather tell the Mistress about the *dovai* and of all the beauty wild Aenan—and, he supposed, the Lake Mother—had brought to those desolate lands. In this sharing, as we know now, was the birth of our times, the Time of Reconciliation. Amarra, being a servitor, knew all the deepest secrets of the Lake Mother's power. She could tell all the Tales of Kheon—the Mother's realm was her domain. Amant, being *dovai*-kith and a son to Lo Dianti, knew more than any Kieldean about wild Aenan, and the *Haaimikin Oide* survived in his memory. Out of that, the two began to make the world whole together.

The Ebsters, who had once been strong and helpful to the Kields, had grown haughty and greedy; the servitors, who had once been so beloved, had become feared; and the kith of wild Aenan, the desert riders who had once traded peaceably with the Kield folk and who had once been revered as Aenan's children, had become outcast. But Amant and Amarra, in their sharing, began to heal the world.

As they talked, they did not notice the short winter's day wane until Emrack appeared with a bowl of stew and bread for all of them. He set the tray down on the floor and took the chair for himself. Amant passed around the food, his heart so full and light he thought he must be shining, as the wishing stone had shone the night the servitors had visited the Academe.

Emrack frowned good-naturedly and said, "Amant, have you practiced the music I taught you yesterday? I have not heard one note of music escape this room."

"No," said the Mistress. "He would have played for me, but I kept him from it." She smiled. "It's my fault."

Emrack gazed at his pupil and rubbed his chin. "I see," he said. "Well, then, you must play now. Go on."

Amant picked up his viola. Setting his chin against the instrument, he tuned and then played through the lullaby Emrack had given him to learn. The orphic fell asleep, snoring noisily, but Amant did not notice because he went from the lullaby on into *Wild Aenan's Lament*.

The Mistress began to sing softly along with the viola. Yet, she did not sing the Lament that he knew—she sang those words that he had heard Osei sing, the first time he had seen her in the Academe. When he finished playing, he asked, "What song were you singing?"

The Mistress touched her finger to her lips and pointed to Emrack. She whispered, "Don't wake him."

"But," he whispered back, "what song were you singing?"

"That was *Trost's Lament,* for her lost child. Isn't it the song you were playing?"

"No. I played *Wild Aenan's Lament.*"

She sat up. "Is that a song from the *dovai*?"

"An Ebster song," he said. "Oeta taught me."

She shook her head. "I've never heard it . . . does it have words?"

"Yes," he said, and began to sing them for her.

"Wait," she said. She stood up with some difficulty, went to the corner table, and took out a paper and ink. Stiffly, she sat at the table and said, "Speak the song—I wish to write it down."

He walked over and stood behind her, as he began to tell the song without singing it. But he stopped short, when he saw that the Mistress had written this:

$$?\sim\eta(\wedge\sim0\sim b7\sim b\sim\eta b\eta((6\sim$$
$$6\sim7\varepsilon\vartheta()($$

Aghast and silent, he stared at what she had done.

"Amant? What's wrong?"

"You can't," he stammered. "Nobody can. I mean, the Ebsters said it was forbidden to write. . . ." He trailed off; remembering that she was a servitor. Servitors need not obey the Ebsters' rule. Then, he said, "Will you teach me? Please?" His voice cracked and dropped an octave. "Please?" He stared at the strange letters on the paper and thought that he had finally found a way to remember all of the *dovai*! He might write out the *Haaimikin Oide*

and everything, all the songs of the steppes—even
his own songs! He could write his own songs, in
the language of the people he loved so. . . .

He began to beg her to teach him in the Mother's
tongue, telling her of all the things he could write
down, if only she would show him how to do it.
"ᐸᐱᒐᐁᑫ,ᒣᐃᐃᐅᐁᑫᐤᒐᐅᐅᑕᐤᑕᐤ," he said.

"Amant!" she cried, stopping him mid-sentence.
She was staring at him, her pale eyes wide in
disbelief. "How can you speak in Trost's own words?
The Ebsters don't know her speech; they only
know how to sing. Where did you learn?"

"In the *dovai*. . . ." He swallowed and touched
his finger to the dried ink of the words on the
paper. "In the *dovai*, we spoke in Aenan's language. I thought, being a servitor, you would know
it. You have written it down, my words. . . ." He
found himself beginning to cry. "The Ebsters sang
it, but they sang it without knowing, without
feeling, and they would not write it; they said
it could not be done. I haven't had anybody to
talk to since before Death came to the *dovai*,
riding on the backs of the corsairs. I thought
I would never speak it again, to anyone." He
looked at her with hope. "Can you . . . do you
speak the tongue? Or do you only know how to
write it?"

The Mistress took his hand in hers and said,
"ᐁᑕᐅᒐᐃᒧᐁᐱᑕᐅᒐᐃ," which translates,
roughly, "Be comforted, child."

Hearing her voice softened and molded by the
shape of his childhood tongue was like hearing a
special song; it brought back his *dovai*-mother's
face to him and his *dovai*-sisters' giggling selves.

" ᔱᐁᖃ ," he said, " ᐊᐁᔭᓯ(ᐊ()ᑕᐧᒡ ," which means, "Ah, I have come home again."

And so did they speak, both haltingly because they were unused to speaking the Mother's tongue aloud. And as late afternoon turned to evening, Amant began to tell Amarra more about the Lo Dianti, and about the ways of the *dovai.* She asked him again about the *dowanaten,* and although it troubled him and still frightened him, he told her what little he had learned from his *dovai*-father and uncle.

At last, she said, "You know, Amant, the servitors have been for many, many a seasonchange the only guardians of Trost's power. Perhaps it is time this is altered."

"What?" he said, startled. "Why?"

She shook her head. "I don't know yet. But you mustn't lose your *dowanaten.*"

He frowned. "I cannot be a servitor. I am not an Ebster. What can I use *dowanaten* for?"

"You will see, I think, in time. And right now . . . I have told you. For Osei's sake. . . ."

"Told me what? What can I do? You haven't told me that. You say to find the girl I first met. But how? And why? What will finding her bring? I've tried talking to Osei. I've tried to make her see. . . ."

"Amant?" said Osei.

Both the Mistress and Amant looked up at the sound of Osei's voice. She stepped into the study and tiptoed up to her sleeping father.

Amant jumped to his feet. "Osei," he whispered.

His sister-cousin looked to him, then back to her father, then to him again. Abruptly, she ran to Amant and hugged him, saying, "I don't know! I don't know what to do!"

He knelt and held her, rocking her in his arms. "Let me help you," he said. "Show me how."

"O!" she cried and shook her head. She pulled away from him and sat next to her father's legs, leaning against the chair, and closed her eyes. "I only know one way. But I'm scared."

"Not that way," said Emrack. He had waked, and he bent over to help lift his daughter to his lap. The fever was beginning to take hold of him. His hands shook and his face was sweaty, but he held Osei tight until she had curled next to him in the chair. He said then, "Let me go, child. Let me go to the Sea."

"No," she whimpered. "No, no, no."

Amant rocked back on his heels. Through his tears, he watched Osei and said nothing, though silently, quietly, he tried to tell himself that he must do as the Mistress said. He had to find a way, through his *dowanaten,* to reach Osei and end the bargain his aunt had forged. But, as he thought on this, he understood that this way would lead him to Death's realm. For he would have to go to the Shore of Sansel's Net, even as Amarra had done, and confront Death, himself. He would have to go back to the empty, roiling Sea and the flat bronze beach, and he would have to find Osei there. Once found, he would lead her back to life. He would use the strength the Lake Mother and wild Aenan had given him, and he would defy Death. If he could. He began to shiver. What if he drowned, as he almost had when Osei had drawn him to the Shore with her?

Amant knew what he had to do. Yet he feared that he could not do it, that he had not the strength. And so he stared at the rug and rocked himself on his heels and said nothing, as the night deepened.

10
An Orphic

WINTER HAD COME and winter had gone and still did Osei linger in Death's shadow. Amant would no longer speak of her choice, though it lay like a stone upon his soul, heavy and unturned. He thought and thought about trying to visit the Shore of Sansel's Net, to find Osei there and perhaps make her return with him. He thought of asking Amarra how he might do this thing—but was it right? Should he interfere with Osei? Even the Mistress had said that Osei must decide for herself. But he knew too that if he were brave enough to use his *dowanaten* and find his way to the Shore, he might discover a way to help his sister-cousin, a way that only would become clear once he took the risk and used the insight.

However, he was terrified—not of the Shore, nor even so much of the *dowanaten*. What he feared was Death. When he had last been on the Shore, with Osei, he had almost joined the Sea himself, instead of helping her at all. What if that happened again? What if Death should take him before his time?

But, he reasoned with himself, young people did die. Had he not almost been lost to the world when the sky-painted coiler had spied him as prey? Perhaps it might be his time now anyway. Perhaps he was meant to lose his life in trying to help Osei. Who could know what the future held? He could only find out by doing, by living through it. Or not. But still he hesitated and wondered and searched his heart in agony. The winter passed by in indecision for him. Yet they were not all unhappy days. They were days of hard work. He was learning much from Emrack.

Now it happens that every spring, even unto our time of Reconciliation, the Drake of Kheon Kield holds a fest. This fest is made in order to give thanks to the Lake Mother for bringing the green leaves and ending Death's winter reign. And all the Kield rejoices in the coming of the spring. Much music is made. Much food is prepared and shared among the households of the Cape. Indeed, all over Gueame are there similar fests because the springtime is sweet to all people, whether they live in the mountain passes of Oron or in the land of a thousand lakes. My great-grandfather used to say that his father remembered such a fest in the *dovai* as well.

The Drake of Kheon would open her summer villa beside the sea to her people during the fest days and nights. Each night there was a different sort of gathering: one night for painters, one for marketeers, one for dancing and music, and one for all the chanters, orphics, and jongleurs, to mention a few. In the days before Amant had come to the Academe, the teachers of that school were the glory of the song-fest night.

"We were proud of our skill and our students," said Emrack, as he helped Amant dress in the fest clothes he had made for his pupil. They were in the orphic's austere chamber, standing beside the window that overlooked the cliffs and field. A procession of high-dressed people—singers all, thought Amant as he watched them—were wading across the grass to the narrow tracks that led down to the beach. They were heading for the Drake's summer villa, that enormous gray-stone building Amant had often wondered about as he had walked in the field, pacing back and forth with the weight of his thoughts.

"We will be proud again," said the orphic firmly.

Amant smiled and turned away from the window, to fold back his new jacket's bell-like sleeves.

"You will be my ears," Emrack continued. "And Oeta's, too. You must do us both that favor tonight." He tightened the leather clasps that lined the front section of the jacket and adjusted the pockets for the young man. "If you sing well, you will find students there tonight—young chanters to give new life to the Academe. And young teachers too, so that the Academe can start to become what it once was."

Amant straightened his shoulders and combed back his hair. It had gotten somewhat thicker over the winter; his beard had begin to grow in too, dark but very fine. That morning, he had cropped it short for the first time, grooming himself for the fest. He had grown a little taller since the autumn—not tall, but enough so that Emrack did not look down to him when they spoke.

The orphic fussed over Amant's robe a few moments longer. Then, he handed the young chanter his viola box, saying, "Before you go, you ought to make a wish. To the Lake Mother—for well-being and success."

Amant rubbed the curves of the carven tree on the top of his viola box. "No," he said. "After the fest, then I will make my wish. After the fest I will speak to the Lake Mother."

"After?" The orphic sat down at his desk.

The young man nodded. "I do have something to ask. But . . . not now. I want to succeed at the fest by myself, using my own talents and my own skill."

Emrack sighed. "You would succeed by yourself, whether you wish to the Lake Mother or no. Trost cannot grant you more talent than you have, but she would, perhaps, look more kindly upon your singing if you wished. But no matter. Ask her when you will, for whatever it is that is on your mind." He smiled a troubled smile and went over to the window and looked out. "You have been singing a lot, have you not?" he said.

Amant laughed. "You've been spying on me?"

"O, I've seen you, out on the hillside there, singing to the wind. And how does your voice sound now? Have you a man's voice altogether, or does it crack still?"

"It is not too strong. It breaks now and then, this tenor of mine. But tonight I hope I will sing true."

"Let me hear you."

"I. . . ."

"Sing the 'Laments'," said Emrack. He faced his pupil. "Please. I can't be at the fest tonight, but I would hear you sing." There was an urgency to his request that startled Amant, a need that swept aside any excuses. The young man took a deep breath and sang the 'Laments'—both wild Aenan's and the Lake Mother's—concentrating on his pitch. He did not sing out fully, nor in the language of the *dovai*, but kept a tight control so that he would not strain his voice. He listened to himself, his eyes closed, and he was pleased to hear that, by the Mother's granting and Aenan's pleasure, he would yet be able to give throat to his music that night before the Drake.

The 'Laments' ended; Amant opened his eyes.

Emrack nodded slowly and said, "Well done. It is good to hear an orphic's skill used so well."

"An orphic," said Amant, under his breath. "Yes." This was the first time Emrack had ever used that title for him, and the young man was deeply, deeply touched. He thought of Oeta and wished the Ebster could have heard him, too.

"Amarra's waiting," said Emrack. He gestured at the young man that it was time for him to leave. "The fest," he said. "Hurry, now."

Amant put his viola down on top of the littered desk and embraced his teacher. He kissed the man's cheek, and then, with a reluctance he couldn't quite understand, he left the room.

In the courtyard of the Academe, Amant sought out the Mistress. That spring's eve was unusually warm. Many night-tongues, their vines clinging to the top of the wall, had opened, scenting the air with their musky, sweet breath. He paced, restless. After a few turns around the courtyard, he stood still, wondering if he shouldn't go back inside and fetch Amarra. Then Nykall appeared, to keep him company. The teka sat between the night-tongues and watched him as he began to pace anew.

The door to the house opened.

"Amarra?" he said, turning toward the sound.

But instead of the Mistress, he saw a child—a girl, all dressed in winter clothes, despite the spring's warmth. She peeped out at him and then ran across the mosaic face of wild Aenan, to stand quite close to him.

He knew the child; it was Osei, that child-Osei whom he had met when he was new to Kheon, that child-Osei whom Amarra had told him to seek out, using his *dowanaten*. But he had not called her—she had simply appeared.

Trembling, he did not move. He was afraid she would disappear, as she had that day when they had played with the ball together. He glanced once, swiftly, at the wishing stone, wondering if the child had come to end Giolla's bargain and wish herself into Death's abode completely. He judged the distance between himself and the stone, and thought he could stop her, if she had come to the yard for that purpose.

But the child did not seem to notice the stone. She kept her gaze upon him. To his surprise, she seemed to be waiting for him either to say something or do something. So, he did. He asked, "Where have you been? I haven't seen you in such a long time—Osei?"

"Shhh . . ." she whispered. "I have a present for you."

"For me? Osei?"

"Shhh . . ." said the child. "You shouldn't call me by her name. She might hear you, and then I would have to go."

He knelt to her on one knee, eye to eye. It was then he noticed that her eyes were not the silver-pale color he had grown accustomed to; rather, they were pale brown, amber-brown, as he remembered them from childhood. He said, "Who will hear me?"

"She might hear you. And if she did, then I would have to go and hide again." The child seemed troubled, and she gazed down at her clenched hand. "I have to hide, you know," she said. "I have to, because she wants me to go away. She doesn't like, much, to remember me."

"Why? Aren't you Osei, too?"

The girl nodded slowly. "I guess. But I think she's forgotten."

"No, no. She's tried to. She can't."

The child grinned. "*I* don't like to hide all the time, in that place where she makes me go." She squinted up at him. "It's a terrible place: a long, empty beach and a black sea. She wants us to stay there all the time."

"And you don't want to stay there, eh?"

"No."

"But Osei makes you stay."

"Yes."

"And what is *your* name?"

She glanced around and whispered, "Osei, of course."

"Of course!" he said, nodding. But he was shivering inside now even more. He didn't know why she had come to him, tonight, on her own, or how she had managed to separate from the part of her that wished to be Death's handmaiden, but he knew this was his opportunity to help her return from the Shore for once and for all. Mastering his fear, he said, "Osei . . ."

"Shhh . . ." she said. "Hold out your hand."

He frowned with impatience. "What . . ." he said, "like this?" He put his hand out, palm upward, expecting something like a stone or a shell or a sweet—something a child would hoard as a little gift.

She dropped a smooth, bumpy, warm something —what was it? he wondered. It made a clackety-clack as it landed in his palm. He looked. . . .

It was his abacus. The abacus that his true father, Lent, had given him, before the night Bildron burned. Its tiny, mystery stones reminded him of so much that, for a moment, he did not move or speak. He wondered at the power of such simple things as a wooden abacus or an old, unstrung violin, things that had no life of their own, yet had the power to bring life to the past, things that seemed to have a touch of *dowanaten*, despite their ordinary faces.

"Thank you," he whispered. He looked up. She had walked a few paces off and was staring up at the teka on the wall.

"Nykall!" he called, and the animal yawned, stretched, and leaped, gliding from her perch among the night-tongues to Amant's feet. She had grown much since he had found her, indeed she had grown from a pup to fullsize, and her silvery neck ruff had changed from down to the white of an adult.

"Death's clarion," said the child. She stepped backward and glanced at Amant with a frightened, worried look. "Don't," she said. "Don't go to the Shore."

Startled, he bent down and stroked the teka's head.

"See?" he said. "She's not going to hurt you. She isn't going to take anyone to the Shore." He picked the creature up. Nykall mewled quietly.

The child drew near to him, until she stood again at his side. She put out her hand and petted the teka, saying, "I thought Death's clarion had come to sing you down to the Sea. They do, you know. They sing out for the souls who are bound for the sea."

"Yes," he said. "I've heard that they do. But Nykall is not always Death's clarion—I don't think she's ever sung for Death."

"Not yet," said the child. "Not yet. Because she's been only a pup. But she will."

He frowned. "Perhaps."

"She scared me. I thought perhaps Death had come for you, too."

Taken aback, he crouched down beside her again and said, "Why would that happen? Is it my . . . is it my time?"

"No. No." She shook her head.

Swallowing his fear, he said, "Is it yours, then?"

She folded her arms and shook her head slightly, a gesture that made her seem wise beyond her years. She said, "It is my choice."

Feeling oddly betrayed and angry, he said. "You mustn't choose to die before you have even lived, Osei." He felt the tears start, and he held onto her shoulders. "Please, please, come home. . . ."

At that moment, the courtyard door opened. Amant glanced around, fearing that his sister-cousin had heard her second self and had come to stop him from helping them both.

But it was Amarra, now, who stepped out of the villa. Glad, and anxious, he turned back to the child whom he held. She was watching the Mistress, too. Then she leaned forward, kissed Amant, and was gone, like smoke. One moment he had been holding her, and in the next he held air. He felt the shock of her loss run through him, and he pounded his fists on the mosaic stone.

Amarra ran up to him and knelt beside him. "She's gone again?"

"Why?" he cried, through clenched teeth. "Why didn't she wait?"

"She'll come back," said Amarra. She stood and walked to the wishing stone. She put her hand on top of the stone and stared up at the night-tongues on the wall, where Nykall had settled herself again.

Amant watched the Mistress, wishing she had not interrupted. He said, "I didn't seek her out, she simply appeared tonight. And you've gone and chased her off."

Amarra shook her head. "She'll come back, Amant. If you wish it."

Amant stood. He walked over to Nykall, and the teka leaped to the ground by his feet. He turned and faced the Mistress. She looked very much the servitor. Her hair was braided and rolled into a coil at the nape of her neck; one white bloom, a night-tongue, slim and only just opening, was tucked into the braid-coil; her silver earrings were complemented by a slight, silver chain on which she had strung a flat face of a silver owl, its eyes and beak inlaid with onyx. She wore black trousers and a blouse of the same fabric, but over these she wore a sleeveless tunic of raw amber silk. He had not seen her so dressed since the night she had called her sister-servitors to the Academe, to help her seek Death. He said, with some surprise, "Shall you sing with me, tonight? Shall we be singing together, for the Drake's pleasure?"

She shook her head and smiled. "You are the orphic, young sir!" She gave him a small, respectful bow and straightened. "Emrack has made you into quite a handsome fest chanter, with his needle and thread." She folded her arms and regarded him. "I shan't sing with you at the Drake's villa. Tonight is for you. I am only your guest— your sister, your cousin, your guest, no more. Remember, the Drake invited you, after your private performance for her ci'esti."

"You make me nervous," he said, reaching down to pick up the teka. Nykall dipped away from his hand and scrambled on top of the wishing stone.

"Good!" she said, still smiling. "You should be nervous. Not everyone gets an invitation to the Drake's presence. You will be envied." She laughed gently. "Don't look so glum. You will do well. I know it."

He sighed. "And Osei? How can I sing with a full heart, knowing that she was here, that she almost . . ."

"Amant," said the Mistress. "You can't force the child to make a choice; you can't force her to come back from the Shore. You can only try to show her *why* she ought to. As you have been, by being patient and living your own life well."

"But . . ." he said, puzzled. "You told me I had to use my *dowanaten* to call forth the little one who visited tonight. And I didn't; I didn't use it."

"No?"

He shook his head.

She reached out and touched his shoulder. "You had to have used your insight, Amant, to have seen her at all. That 'child' exists only in the past; your *dowanaten* brings you to that past, allows you to share in it and to see her as she once was—to see that child who has been left behind by Osei."

He shook his head again in confusion.

The Mistress put her arm around his shoulder. "You are *dowanaten*, Amant; it is as much a part of your life as breathing—you only need to learn how to focus it and not fear it."

"If that were true," he said stubbornly, "why did I almost become a teka that night, never to come home again?"

"Because," she said, "you fear your own self, Amant. You fear your own strength and seek to hide from it. Isn't that so?"

He did not answer. He knew what she said was true. Yet still he doubted he could have saved himself that night. He thought that if she had not called him back, he would be a teka even now, roaming the wide skies at Nykall's side.

She hugged him and turned toward the door.

"Come," she said, "We will be late if we don't walk quickly."

He followed after her out of the Academe. They did not speak until they were halfway across the grassy field that led to the path down to the Drake's villa. Then, Amant said, "Tell me, did Aunt Giolla make her bargain with Death in winter?"

"Yes."

"And Osei was about yea high?" He marked off a child's height against his waist.

"Yes, as you saw her tonight."

"You . . . you saw her, too?" He had not thought to ask the Mistress whether she had actually seen the child he had spoken to.

"Yes," said Amarra. "Briefly, before Death visited to urge her back to the Shore."

"Death?" He stopped on the path in surprise.

"Yes." The Mistress turned and frowned. "Did you not see him?"

"No."

The Mistress frowned, but said nothing. She continued down to the villa.

Amant dawdled. He stared up at the starlit sky and the clear, blue half-moon shining on the auburn grass, the narrow dirt track, the quiet field. He suddenly did not want to go on; he did not want to sing; he did not want to face the Drake's crowded villa and fest music. He wanted to stay on the hill, above it all, safe and quiet. Maybe if he stayed there, in the dark, Osei would choose to come to him again and he could snatch her away from Death without ever having to see the Lake Mother's dread sibling. He turned away from the path and faced the Kield.

Somebody was coming down the path after him. A tall, dark woman, dressed as darkly as the Mistress was dressed, hurried along toward the villa behind him. Curious, he waited for her to approach, when Amarra called his name. And so he left before he could speak to the stranger, meaning to look for her when they arrived at the Drake's.

☆

THE DRAKE of Kheon's villa was alight with flame. Floor candles and torches and the brilliant dress of her guests made the hall where the ci'esti entertained the visitors seem alive with fire. Chanters and orphics sat here and there at tables piled with fruit and nut-bowls and decanters of a light yellow wine.

Off to one side of the crowded hall was a porch that looked out to the breakers of the White Sea and the sand of the cove. In the corner of this porch, a tent had been pitched—a large tent of a dark red color that glowed with light from within. The ci'esti sauntered near the tent, guarding the Drake Villae from unwanted intruders. The Drake had come out from her usual seclusion to listen to the invited musicians and to rest. No impassioned pleas were to be heard on fest night—and the ci'esti would see to it that the Drake's rest and pleasure were not disturbed.

At first, Amant and Amarra wandered about the crowd, meeting new people. But Amant quickly tired of this and went to stand on the threshold of the seaporch, to wait his turn to see the Drake. Amarra stood next to him. She spoke little, but pointed out this orphic and that, many who had once been Emrack's pupils, until Amant gave up trying to remember their names. She murmured anecdotes about these musicians until his head fairly spun. She seemed to know them all, but no one seemed to know her.

Finally, the call came for those invited to wait upon the Drake. With a flush of unease and fright, Amant left the Mistress—who smiled her confidence at him—and followed the other musicians. Only five had actually been asked to play directly for the Drake; three of these walked before Amant out to the seaporch. They stood where the ci'esti told them, beside the porch wall, while they led the first of the chanters over to the mouth of the tent. The singer did not go inside, but stayed before the tent and began her performance. Amant listened and glanced back into the hall, where Amarra sat. He wished she would step nearer so that he might speak to her before his turn, but he dared not beckon her across the busy hall.

The night wind was rather sharp, and he hugged himself inside his fest jacket, hoping that his turn would come speedily. He was so nervous, he barely heard the first singer at all. He found himself going over his own music, as a flautist began her piece for the Drake.

Someone grabbed his arm and said, "Mossdon chanter! So you *have* stayed in Kheon! Where have you been? Where have you been hiding that we could not find you all this time?"

Amant caught his breath and turned around. Tio Nary and the other jongleurs stood in a half-circle around him. Tio chuckled and gave the young man a long, easy smile. He said, "We looked for you in Bildron, to give you your share of the night's linganuli. But the porter told us you had left."

"Tio, ask him about . . ." said Tio's sister, Rican.

"Don't be rude," said the drummer. He smiled his easy smile, but his voice had a sharp rebuke in it, and Rican blushed.

Amant glanced about, searching for Amarra. The roundel, however, stood close to him, and he could not see past them into the hall. Uneasy, he began to sidle toward the ci'esti, hoping his turn to play would be soon.

"Where have you been?" said Tio again. "We've asked after you in Kheon, once the porter told us you had arrived here. He said, in fact, that you had come for the Academe. When you found it abandoned, where did you go?"

"I didn't find it abandoned," said Amant in surprise. "I've been at the Academe."

Rican laughed and leaned against her brother. "Surely you've been there—with whom? The mice that live in the rafters? The Academe has been abandoned. We've gone by there looking for you. The yard is full of wretched weeds, and the place is quite, quite empty."

Amant looked from face to face, wondering what they wanted with him, that they had gone so far as to hunt him up at the Academe. He had been afraid they would follow him, after he had abandoned the Pocket, because they had seen a touch of the *dowanaten*, but he had lost that fear a long time ago. Now he could see that his fear had not been so very foolish and that, somehow, through her powerful insight, Amarra had been hiding them all from scrutiny—herself, Amant, Emrack, and Osei. He said nothing and again tried to sidle past the jongleurs. But Tio was vigilant. He stepped closer to Amant and said, "How did you manage to hide from us?"

"I wasn't hiding," said Amant.

"All right, then, how did you manage this?"

"What?" Amant frowned.

"How did you get a sitting for the Drake tonight? You—a newcomer to Kheon. We have been trying for an audience from season to season and never a word did we get from the ci'esti. Then you show here tonight from nowhere, to take our place."

"I have not taken your place," said Amant, angrily. "I have not taken anyone's place! I was invited." He glanced toward the Drake's tent. The ci'esti were praising the last singer, and one of them nodded at him and started to walk toward him. Amant felt his heart leap—it was his turn!

Tio laughed. "Invited—yes. But what I want to know is how you managed to get yourself invited. Whom did you bribe? And what did you use to bribe the ci'esti? They are so difficult even to speak with, much less bribe. I've tried. I can't understand how you managed it. But no matter. You can manage it for us, too."

"What?" said Amant.

Tio grabbed his arm and held onto him, while Rican took his viola case from him. She said, "Sing with us tonight, chanter."

"Let go! Here—give me back. . . ." He reached for his viola, but it was snatched away. Tio shoved the young man roughly against Ne, who grabbed his shoulders.

"Sing with us," said Rican. "We have waited so long to sing for the Drake and win her praise. Every season she has denied us, but now, with you . . . do you know what it will mean for us? Linganuli from every hand in every Kield. We can call ourselves the Drake's own favorites, the only jongleurs ever to sing for her pleasure! You must sing with us tonight, little chanter," she said, her voice getting harsh. "The ci'esti beckon you now and will be displeased if you keep them waiting any longer."

Helpless, Amant walked between the brother and sister toward the tent. The others followed. He wanted to speak against the roundel and tell the ci'esti, but Tio had his hands on Amant's shoulders and Rican still had his viola.

When they had reached the mouth of the tent, the ci'esti nodded for them to begin. The players found themselves alone on that seaporch, except for the tent and the ci'esti, and they were confused—where was the Drake? They complained that they had not come to sing for the ci'esti, but for the Drake!

Amant stepped away from the roundel, as far as he dared. Let them complain, he thought. He knew that the Drake was there in the tent, unseen but present. He could feel her strangeness vibrating on the air, as an insect's wing; he could taste her strangeness—it tainted the salt wind. He was glad, indeed, that the tent stood between him and her strangeness. He had heard rumors and bits of tales that said the Quedahl Drakes all were only half-human. Feeling as he did at that moment, he did not doubt the rumors.

He took another step away from the jongleurs.
Rican held his viola, but he decided he would not
need it. He would rely on himself, on his voice
only. He took another step. Tio made a motion
toward Amant, as if to stop him, so he did not
wait any longer, but began to sing the *Song of the
Little Owl.*

Caught off guard, the jongleurs remained silent
for a moment. Then, reluctant to forfeit their
chance before ci'esti—and perhaps the Drake, they
did not know—they began to follow Amant's lead.
But they could not sing as a roundel, as they were
accustomed, because Amant had started. They gave
instead a limping chorus made even more lame by
the fact that, while they sang the melody as a
nonsense luilaby, Amant sang it with feeling and
in an accent that was at odds with the roundel's.

Amant caught a glimpse of Tio Nary's face as
the lullaby drew to a close. The fury that he saw in
the man's posture and in his furrowed, thick brows
and sharply drawn, thin lips, made Amant take
another hasty step away from the group. He bowed
to the ci'esti (and to the hidden Drake) and, before the *Song of the Little Owl* finished out, he
began another melody:

Fire, my beloved, and I the earth's child . . .

His song, his own music—the jongleurs were forced,
one by one into silence. He sang the whole once
through and then switched into the language of
his people, and the tongue of the Lake Mother,
which the Mistress had taught him how to write:

He sang full-throated, as a bird caught up by the absolute joy of dawn. But then, suddenly, he felt that he was not alone in the singing. Had one of the jongleurs joined him? How? He looked around for the singer and found Amarra. She stood next to him and echoed his words so that their voices twined and meshed, as the viola and bass flute parts of the song might mesh and twine. Smiling, he sang to her. He held out his hands, but before he could clasp hers, he heard yet a third voice. . . .

Osei!

Sweet and high and light, her voice darted into the song swift and smooth. And he recognized that voice not only as hers, but also as the voice that had taught him words to the *Song of the Smoke Bamboo,* the voice inside him. She stood on the seaporch. He saw her there, the same child who had given him the gift of his abacus. Yet now she wore no winter clothes but a white nightdress, much like the one the other Osei, the older girl, often wore. Her child's eyes shone as silvery as the teka's once silver ruff. She sang the last verse with Amarra and Amant softly, hesitantly, as if she feared the music. Her soprano was as clean and as ringing as the tones of the Ling chimes, and her voice grew stronger with each note.

He knew, he sensed, that no one could see his sister-cousin but himself; no one else could hear her—except Amarra. He knew, he sensed, that she had come here to bid them both a final farewell. Desperate, his whole self charged with his desire to call her back from Death's side, he turned toward her and sang to her . . .

Rain, my beloved, and I the earth's child . . .

pouring every ounce of himself into the melody and the words. He felt a queer, dissolving sensation; he fragmented, split into a thousand selves, but still one self, as a cloud seems all one, yet is made up of a condensation of many, as a song sounds whole but is made of many notes. He became those notes, he became the rain, and he washed over Osei, insinuating himself into her dreams, calling her home.

She glanced up, her face wet with the rain or her tears, he could not tell. He found himself standing next to her, whole once more, and he knelt, holding out his hands.

She took a step. Another. Then another.

He felt as if his body were holding its breath, although he sang on, sang for her life and his.

She touched his hands with her own, calling to him, and then, suddenly, they were alone, together on the Shore.

He gasped. Bewildered, he stood, his heart emptied by the music, and his desire to help Osei. She stood next to him, and she was no longer the child to whom he had been singing, but full-grown. She looked at him with her silvery, servitor's eyes, and her face was still wet with tears.

The wind blew steadily and mournful around them, and the flat, brassy light made Osei seem to him again like a statue of gold and diamond. Yet, the statue cried, and this time, he knew where he was and he did not fear. He took her hands in his and began to sing, again.

His voice sounded reedy to him, thinned out by the unrelenting emptiness of the Shore. The moaning wind tried to silence him, as did the Sea's endless murmuring whisper. The whisper of the Sea began to grow as he continued his singing; as it grew, Osei trembled and cried even more and nestled closer to her cousin, seeking warmth and seeking his strength.

As he put his arm around Osei's waist, and tried to lead her up the flat sand and away from the Sea's black murmurs, he saw a stranger running down the beach after them. The stranger was tall and dark. With a start, Amant recognized the woman he had seen following him to the Drake's villa.

Osei saw the stranger, too, and she jumped away from Amant's embrace, to stand between him and the tall stranger.

Then, he knew. The one who smiled at them now, her dark face unreadable in the cool, rayless light, was Death. She was terribly thin, and her eyes were as silver as Osei's, as silver as Amarra's. She stood near the water's edge, dressed in shadows, holding her arms out to Osei, who tottered visibly and then stood irresolute. Death said nothing, nor did she beckon. She waited.

Amant wanted to scream, but he did not. He wanted to rush at Osei, grab her, carry her forcibly away. But he didn't. He knew she had to make her choice, now. And so he too waited; but as he waited for her, he began to sing again. This time, he sang the 'Laments', intertwining the verses of the two, singing of loss and sorrow and hoping that his sister-cousin would hear.

Osei slowly turned to look at him. She glanced swiftly back at the Sea. And then she looked straight up overhead. She closed her eyes and she too sang.

The sound of her voice on the Shore seemed to shatter the world. Amant heard a long, low shrieking whistle, and the Sea seemed to leap up at him and the sand seemed to shift under him. He reached for Osei's hand and held it, and they sang together for an instant before they sank. . . .

Amant found himself on the seaporch of the Drake's villa. He wasn't sinking. The Shore was gone, and so was Osei. Yet, his heart was strangely peaceful. Osei had vanished from the Drake's porch, but he knew she had come back from the Shore, that she had made her choice to live when she chose to sing with him in that place where music could not live. Distantly, as if he were half-asleep, he heard the ci'esti praise his song. He barely paid them heed, because he saw Amarra at the porch's edge, leaning out over the wall into the darkness, toward the White Sea below. She did not look at him. He saw her profile, softened by the moonlight, yet her face was tense and still. How rigidly she stood! She appeared to be listening.

He called to her softly. He wanted to say, "Osei is home!" but at that very instant, he understood why she could not look at him or respond. He remembered what Osei's choice would mean to Emrack. And as he watched the Mistress, she climbed up onto the seaporch's wall and lifted her arms. Wings spread out from her shoulders, dark feathers rustling in the wind. Then, an owl rose into the night sky. It drifted over the sea. She was gone.

And Amant knew—O! he knew!—that the owl was off on a long journey tonight, to that same place from which he had just returned. Osei had made her choice. Death would visit the Academe.

Stricken with grief, he whispered, "Emrack . . ." as he watched the great owl sail off toward the east. He knew where Amarra was heading, because a servitor of Trost must always aid a soul on its path to the Sea of Sansel's Net. He silently wished Emrack an easeful journey.

Soon, the ci'esti, full of praise for the new orphic, led Amant off the terrace, to introduce him to the others in the hall again, and to make it known that the Drake was more than well pleased. The jongleurs followed, like dogs after a meal, silent and sullen.

Amant went meekly, half-heartedly listening to the ci'esti's talk and trying to ignore the jongleur's jealous, insincere praise. Tio glared at the young orphic with open hatred, but my great-great-grandfather did not really notice. He had something else to think about because, faroff; above the sounding the White Sea's waves, he heard Death's clarion—his Nykall—cry, "keir-ah!"

✩

NOW, as many people know, and as it is written in the annals of Kheon, that spring fest at which my great-great-grandfather sang the *Song of the Smoke Bamboo* was much spoken of and remembered. Kieldeans far and wide, in every part of

Gueame, heard the news that the Academe had a new, orphic, Ebster-trained, as a teacher.

Thus, Amant found himself asked by more than a few youngsters if he would not open the Academe to them. And, in time, new teachers of great skill came to his doorstep. As the Tales of the Reconciliation tell us, my great-great-grandfather built the Academe back into the grand school that it was, grander, I think, than it had been in Emrack's day.

But before even one new student had appeared, before Amant even thought about opening the Academe as a school, during that summer after the spring fest, Osei returned home. She made a slow return, since the illness that had afflicted Emrack now afflicted her. For most of the spring, in fact, she was ill; her soul's sojourn on the Shore had left her body weak. Amant and Amarra nursed her, and as the days grew warmer, so did Osei grow stronger.

One summer day, when the sunshine poured out onto the courtyard and the front garden of the Academe like a flood of warm honey, Amant stepped out of the front door and stood under the yew tree beside a curtain of young, green grass. Among the shoots at his feet sat a little stone statue of a frog, its wide eyes mildly watching the garden around it. Amant seated himself on a flat rock near the frog and closed his eyes, letting the sun warm his face and thinking about Osei. The thought of her filled him with as much sunshine as filled the garden—maybe more.

In a few moments, he heard the front door open again. Amarra stepped out, carrying a basket covered with a cloth. A few slim night-tongues thrust out from beneath the cloth. She stopped on the slate path and turned, speaking. But Amant could not hear what she said. He stood up.

Osei walked out onto the porch gingerly. She squinted and pushed her curly hair back off her face.

He sprinted across the lawn to her and offered her a hand. She took it and stepped from the house to the grass. She was thin, and she was not a child now but a young woman, the Osei she would have been if she had not lived, in part, as Death's handmaid. Her dark skin had a healthy flush beneath its cinnamon color, and she gripped his hand strongly. Her icy, clear eyes, servitor's eyes, regarded him fondly. She took a few more steps, and then Amant picked her up and ran over to the garden gate with her.

She laughed and said, "Put me down!" And so he did. She opened the gate and solemnly led her companions into the street.

The three made their way along the crowded paths, as the sun climbed past noon and the day became a lazy, hot afternoon. Amant unlaced his jacket's collar and watched Osei. She seemed well, curious about all that they saw, asking questions as they went along, her arm lightly resting on his.

The field beside the sea hummed with fat bees that had strayed from the Drake's apiaries on the adjoining hills. As they settled themselves in the sand just beyond the grasses, Amant glanced back at the graveyard far above them. The black stones were nearly hidden by the summer growth, but he could make out the one clear spot and the new stones that he had placed there. Still, the grass had encroached on the mound of dark loam; the new stones, three smooth sea stones he had dragged up the hill from the beach, seemed less strange to him now and more a part of the earth.

Amarra began to unpack their food from the covered basket. Osei wriggled out of her pants and shirt. Amant did the same, piling his clothes in a concave nest for Nykall, who then landed with a thump near his bare feet. He laughed and picked her up. Full-grown, the teka was not so much larger than when he had found her abandoned in Bildron, but she was far stronger. She wriggled from his grasp and sniffed at the nest of his clothes.

"You'll find sand in your shirt and pants for weeks," said Amarra. "Look at that animal, look what she's doing!"

Nykall was feathering her "nest" with sand.

He laughed and patted the creature on her flat head. "I don't mind."

Amarra shook her head, smiling. "You will when you try to put those pants on again."

He shrugged and glanced around. "Where did Osei go?"

"With the flowers—up there." The Mistress pointed to the graveyard.

He sighed and nodded. He moved, as if to follow his sister-cousin, when Amarra said, "Stay. She needs some time to herself. I think she's tired of her nursemaids, and this is the first time she has been to the grave."

"Yes," said Amant absently. Thinking about Emrack saddened him still. He missed his teacher and had no words for the emptiness Emrack's absence brought.

Amarra took off her shoes and sighed. Then, she said, "Osei is much herself, now. She won't need a nursemaid, soon."

He glanced at her. "What do you mean?"

"I mean, it's time that I should be going."

"Going," he repeated flatly, stunned. "Why?"

"I am a servitor," she said, gently. "You know this. Trost's servitors are bound to wander Gueame, answering the wishes of the Lake Mother's children. It's time I should look to my *own* children."

"But . . . but you've been here. All this time. . . ."

"Yes—to help Osei end her bargain with Death. Osei and Giolla are my sisters. I came here to help them, and stayed to see Osei's decision, whatever it would be. To persuade her, if I could, to live. But she is well now. And I must do as the Mother asks me to. Besides, I have much to learn, also."

"About the insight?"

"Yes. And about myself."

He rummaged through the basket and took out a cluster of purple-eyed berries to hide his confusion. He broke a few off the stem and gave them to her. "I hoped you were going to stay . . . I mean, I never thought you would leave."

"I know."

"And you won't?"

She sighed and rolled the berries around in the palm of her hand. "The Academe is not my home, Amant. I became its Mistress, at Emrack's request and because Osei needed me. But I am a servitor, and must travel where my soul sends me, as one day Osei, too, must do, when she is ready to take her mother's place."

"Is it . . . is it what you want to do?"

"Yes."

He sat very, very still on the blanket, staring at the fruit in Amarra's hand. The sun felt too warm on his skin. The bees seemed suddenly to drone with a terrific force. He attempted to gather his wits, and he said, as quietly as he could manage, "But, I love you, Amarra. What will Osei and I do without you?" He wondered if his heart was going to fall out. But it stayed in his chest, thumping madly.

She smiled and brushed his hair back from his forehead, so that she could see his face. She made him look at her, and she shook her head. "You and Osei don't need me anymore."

"But . . ."

"And I love you, too. Always." She sounded both tender and amused.

"Then stay," he said, stubbornly.

"Amant," she scolded, "the Academe is yours."

He glanced away. Had the sun gone? The air felt cool, and the breeze was rather chilly. He shooed the teka off her makeshift nest and shook the sand from his shirt. He did not know what to say or do; he felt both chided and angry as he struggled into his shirt, tearing it a little in his haste and confusion.

"Amant!" cried Osei. She was running down the grassy hill toward the blanket. Her little feet scattered sand in all directions. "Amant! Come down to the sea! I want to swim, but I'm afraid to jump in by myself. Please?" She ran on, her thin arms pumping up and down, her elbows shooting out from her sides.

He was about to tell her no, that she should rest and that it was too cold to go swimming, when the Mistress stood and called out—"We're coming!"

Frustrated, he pushed himself to his feet. He peeled off his shirt for the second time, grabbed a spare blanket, and marched down the beach toward his sister-cousin. The teka followed him, springing along over the dune grass, until she caught a wing tip on a tall stalk and toppled over. As he lifted her out of the grass, she shook all over, as if she had gotten wet or as if she were expressing indignation at his interference. This demonstration disrupted his ill humor, and he had to laugh.

"Have you been on this beach before?" asked Osei. She stood next to him, hands on her hips, breathing hard from her run. Her bare toes were caked with damp sand.

"No," he said. "Not here. Over there." He pointed to the Drake's villa at the far end of the cove. "Don't you remember?"

"Remember?" She frowned. "I don't remember that villa, no. But this beach!" Her face was alight. "It's so beautiful! I don't think I've ever seen a place so beautiful." She sighed contentedly and gazed down to the water.

"Never?" he asked; he remembered how she had said the Shore of Sansel's Net seemed beautiful to her.

"Never, ever." She held her hand out to him and smiled. "I had forgotten what the shore is supposed to feel like, this light wind and the sun's warmth." She closed her eyes and took a deep breath. "And the salty taste of the air. Everywhere, I find shells and can hear the birds crying about the fast fish they are chasing, out there. . . ." She pointed toward the horizon where the sun's light danced on the choppy glass of the water. "Take me swimming, will you?"

He held her offered hand and squeezed it. "Why did you come home finally, Osei? I thought . . . I almost thought I would lose you, that night on the Shore."

She leaned her head on his shoulder. "It was the music and your love, Amant. I could hear life in the notes of your song and love in the melody, and warmth in the weave of the sound. Death has no song—he hears no music. Do you know I can play the Ling again?"

He shook his head, forcing back his tears. "No," he said, his voice wavering a little. "I didn't know. Will you play for me?"

"Tonight. But come. Let's go in the water, please?"

They started over the sand to the sea. But then, Osei stopped and made him stop also. She turned around and cried to Amarra, "Are you coming in?"

The Mistress cupped her hands around her mouth and called back, "Of course—of course I am!" And, scooping up another small blanket, she dashed across the sand to them. The three then walked in silence toward the water.

Amant did not know what to say or how to speak of what he felt; there was too much boiling up inside him, as turbulent as the fuming ocean

that dashed up on the cove and swirled at his feet.
So, instead of speaking, he lifted Osei suddenly
and spun her around so high off the ground that
she shrieked out giggles and clung to his neck
until he stopped. Laughing, she pinched him, and
he, miming pain, put her down. She jumped away
and clumsily ran from him; Nykall loped beside
her, dabbling a paw now and then in the foam.

"I'll catch you!" he shouted.

"Don't tire her too much," said Amarra.

He turned to the Mistress. She was standing to
her waist in the water, about to make a dive and
swim off. He said, "She will probably tire me."

Amarra laughed. "Yes, I think it so!"

He swallowed. "I will be here, at the Academe.
When you want to come back."

"No," she said. "You will go where your music
takes you. As I must go, now. But you will always
come home. As I will return, someday."

"You will?"

"Did you think I would forget you, cousin? Did
you think I would never wish for you and Osei?"
She folded her arms. "Well!" she said, trying to
sound petulant. "Have you forgotten me already?"

When he hugged her, she hugged him back.
And he did not let her see that he was crying.

☆

SO, THAT IS HOW the boy-who-was-thrown-away
found a true home. Because, as the Mistress pre-
dicted, he always returned to the Academe, after
travels that took him to distant isles. And, as I
have said, the Academe became famous again for
music. Amant's songs brought him respect; his
knowledge brought students to Kheon; and his

wisdom helped to bring wild Aenan's memory back to the Kieldeans, who had woefully forgotten their father. Without that music, perhaps the Reconciliation might never have happened. And what would have become of Gueame? Sometimes I fear that Death would have overtaken Trost's domain, making people distrust one another, making us forget the beauty of wild Aenan and the Lake Mother both.

O, yes, I could sit with you for the whole night and tell you story upon story about my great-great-grandfather—of how he did meet the Drake of Kheon, at last; of how he visited the Ebsters and broke their rigid rules to become one of them. Or I could tell you about his pupils and of the Reconciliation's growth. Or I might even tell you about beautiful Osei and of how she became the Drake of Bildron!

But I will stop here, because we have already traveled together a hard and tortuous way, you and I, a great distance indeed from that muddy, rutted lane where we started. I must go to sleep now, as you would too, if you had told this long story.

What?

Well, of course. Before I sleep, I will tell you one more thing. Let me answer that question I see in your heart. . . .

I was told that, all his long life, Amant Nowaetnawidef had a strange custom he followed whenever he returned to the Academe after a voyage. He would shut himself up in the study, usually with a fire roaring in the hearth, and he would open the window. Soon, they say, a teka would land on the sill. It was not Nykall, no, for Nykall would be curled up by the hearth, asleep already. This teka would leap into the room onto the rug, and then, well, then my great-great-grandfather would have a visitor with him, with whom he spent the night talking and sometimes singing.

And that visitor would come to the Academe, even unto the days when he had grown old and blind, even unto those days when he never voyaged but only sat in the mosaic courtyard and drowsed in the sun. Not many knew her, nor even saw her, because she most often arrived at night, on the wings of the teka she could become. I saw her, once: A graceful woman was she, with strange, pale eyes like Osei's and straight black hair, as black as a teka's coat. I know I need not tell you her name.

Notes

a	(symbol)	m	(symbol)
ĕ	(symbol)	n	(symbol)
î	(symbol)	p	(symbol)
ō	(symbol)	r	(symbol)
û	(symbol)	s	(symbol)
y	(symbol)	t	(symbol)
b	(symbol)	v	(symbol)
c	(symbol)	w	(symbol)
d	(symbol)	x	(symbol)
f	(symbol)	z	(symbol)
g	(symbol)	ch	(symbol)
h	(symbol)	sc	(symbol)
j	(symbol)	gh	(symbol)
k	(symbol)	ea	(symbol)
l	(symbol)		

This is a phonetical rendering of the alphabet of the first language of Gueame. The Ebsters can speak it, but haltingly and badly; the servitors of Trost can speak, read, and write it, although they, too, do not speak it well. The only group of people who spoke it fluently, before the Reconciliation, were the Tenebrians.

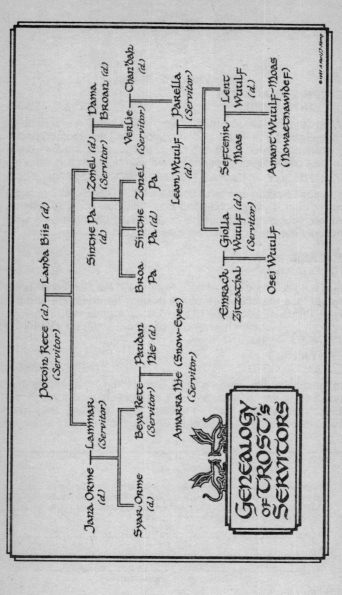

GENEALOGY
of TROSC's
SERVITORS

© 1987 J. Phn / J. R. Stamp

DAW

New Worlds of Fantasy

STEPHANIE A. SMITH
☐ SNOW EYES   (UE2286—$3.50)

When the mysterious mother who abandoned her returns to claim Snow-Eyes for the goddess known as Lake-Mother, Snow-Eyes is compelled to go with her to the goddess' citadel—there to face betrayal and a confrontation with her own true nature.

☐ THE BOY WHO WAS THROWN AWAY (UE2320—$3.50)

The spell-binding sequel to SNOW-EYES! Gifted with a musical magic and a shape-changing talent he can scarcely control, Amant struggles to rescue his cousin caught in a terrifying spell halfway between life and the realm of Lord Death.

MELANIE RAWN
☐ DRAGON PRINCE   (UE2312—$4.50)

In a land on the verge of war, Rohan and his Sunrunner bride would face the challenge of the desert, the dragons—and the High Prince's treachery! *"Marvelous . . . impressive . . . fascinating . . . I completely and thoroughly enjoyed DRAGON PRINCE."* —Ann McCaffrey

TANYA HUFF
☐ CHILD OF THE GROVE   (UE2272—$3.50)

In a land where magic's spell was fading, one wizard had survived to wreak madness and destruction. And through the Elder Races had long withdrawn from mortals, they now bequeathed them one last gift—Crystal, the Child of the Grove!